After wringing out the garments as best I could, I spread them out on the ground in the sun which was still an hour or so short of setting.

Suddenly self-conscious, I strode over to look down on her as she lay waiting for me. She was smiling, a smile of welcome.

"Ralf," she said softly as she looked up at me, "do you realize that today is my eighteenth birthday? Today is the day I was scheduled to have my operation. Then, with a Class Two rating, I would be eligible to be your mate."

Hearing her say these things now, and looking down at her lying there, her lovely body still glistening with beads of water, I realized what a terrible mistake I had made in not telling her earlier that I was not Ralf, her promised one, but Rolf, the mutant.

Her voice went —

"Here we are my love, really together. Tomorrow — who knows what dangers we may be facing. Tonight we have each other. I love you, Ralf. Stay with me. Love me. Do you love me as much as I love you?"

I stumbled for words. "Elissa," I mumbled, "I love you more th~~an life itself.~~" Then I hesitated. Now, if ever, I h~~ad~~

THE FIRST TWELVE
LASER BOOKS

ARTHUR TOFTE

WALLS WITHIN WALLS

Cover
Illustration by
KELLY FREAS

Laser Books

WALLS WITHIN WALLS

A LASER BOOK / first published 1975

© 1975 by Arthur Tofte

ISBN 0-373-72005-X

LASER BOOKS are published by Harlequin Enterprises
Limited, 240 Duncan Mill Road, Don Mills, Ontario M3B 1Z4,
Canada. The Laser Books trade mark, consisting of the words
"LASER BOOKS" is registered in the Canada Trade Marks
Office, the United States Patent Office, and in other
countries.
Printed in U.S.A.

PART ONE

WALLS OF UPPER CITY

I

We could hear the slow, steady beat of marching feet —the watch guard! It was coming our way. . . .

Ralf and I rushed to the small peep-hole our father had built into our solid front gate-door. An inner bracing on the gate allowed us to climb up and peer out.

Ralf got there first. I could see that he was highly excited as he clambered up the bracing and pulled aside the shield that prevented anyone outside from looking into our enclosed yard. He put his eye to the tiny hole.

Even before he slid down to give me a chance to look out, I knew that the watch guard had gone past.

It was not to be this time!

We looked at each other and laughed in relief. The next instant we were in each other's arms weeping.

It was not to be this time. But surely it would happen the next time the watch guard came by. Or the time after that. Another hour? Another two hours?

Ever since Ralf and I had awakened that morning, we were keyed up for what the day would bring. It was our sixth birthday. And in Resurrection City sixth birthdays were very important. That was the date on which children were taken away from their homes and their parents by the watch guard, and given over to the city for training.

As twins, Ralf and I had known of this, had dreaded it, and at the same time were fascinated with it.

We loved our parents. We loved our home. But the mere thought of going out beyond the high wall that surrounded our home . . . to see what life was like in the rest of the city . . . to play with other children—it was almost more than we could imagine.

"Well, Rolf," my twin said to me, "what will we do now? It will be at least an hour before the next watch guard comes by."

Tears welled up again in my eyes. It was unthinkable that Ralf, my other half, would be leaving me. I might never see him again. He was the lucky one.

For weeks Ralf and I had suspected something was wrong. Our mother and father had been unusually kind to us, hugging us more often than ever before, doing little nice things for us.

Even more disturbing than that, several times we had heard our mother weeping and our father trying to comfort her. Yes, we knew something was wrong. And whatever it was, was going to happen on our sixth birthday. And this was that date.

We knew that much. Yet we didn't know what it all meant. We knew that Ralf was going to have to leave us and I would stay. But why?

After breakfast, our parents had tried to explain. All children, they said, were taken away by the city on their sixth birthday. To be educated and trained according to a plan. To serve the city. Those with superior abilities could become eligible to be Class Two leaders. The rest stayed as workers in Class Three.

Our parents, we knew, were Class Three. Ralf, by doing well in the training schedule, could rise to the Class Two rating. They were the managers who reported only to the Class One rulers of the city.

All this meant little or nothing to our six-year old minds. The thing that really upset me was that Ralf and I would be separated. For six years we had never had a moment apart. Now, we might never see each other again.

"Why can't I go too?" I pleaded.

It was then that our mother broke down and couldn't stop crying for several minutes. Later, when she was able to talk again, she told Ralf that if he loved us, he must never tell anyone that he had a twin brother. Never!

To keep her from crying any more, Ralf eagerly agreed.

It was about this time we had rushed to the front gate-door at the sound of the approaching watch guard. After they had gone by, my brother had said, "What will we do now?"

He needn't have asked. We both knew what we wanted most to do.

Although we had never been permitted to leave our yard and venture out onto the street, we had peeked up and down. We could see that all the houses were just like ours. Each one was surrounded by a high brick wall almost twice the height of a man. It was in our side wall that we had discovered some months before where a small section of the bricks had loosened. We had carefully worked out several of the bricks on our side so that we could peep through into the yard next door.

A girl lived there—a beautiful girl, with long, flowing blond hair, red laughing lips and soft pink cheeks, her body slender and yet sturdy. She was a little younger than we were, a month or two at most. But she was our fairy princess, our secret playmate who never knew that we watched her every chance we could get.

She danced for us, not ever knowing we were devouring her with our eyes. She ran, laughing happily, around her yard. She seemed always to be gay and bubbling over with gladness. She played games that were strange to us. And we watched, wishing there was some way to break down the wall that separated us.

Her name was Elissa. We had often heard her mother come to the door and call her. Yes, Elissa, through the past half year had been the playmate we never could have.

Ralf and I moved around to the side wall and quickly removed the loose bricks. We peered through. Yes,

9

Elissa was there. It was a warm day and she was wearing an abbreviated white tunic, a small copy of the standard item of clothing worn by all. Never had she seemed more beautiful than now as she lay stretched out on the ground. She lay on her back with her legs slightly apart. She was looking up at the cloudless sky. Even from where we were, we could hear her singing softly, a hum more than a song.

I could have wept again, looking over at Ralf and thinking this might be the last time he could take the secret look at Elissa, the fair one.

Finally her mother called her and she went into her house. We turned away. After resetting the bricks, we started to go back toward the house. Instead, however, Ralf headed around to the back. I followed. Our father had told us one time that our property was exactly the same as all the other Class Three houses in the city. But for all our six years it had been our whole world. We had seen nothing else.

Ralf went around touching things. The rows of corn that were just beginning to tassle. The tomato plants. The cabbage and lettuce and carrots and beans. He and I had helped plant the seeds, had weeded and nurtured the growing things. It was ours as much as it was our parents. And Ralf was leaving it all.

The wall around our house was ours too. Although most of it was built before we were past the baby stage, we had watched our father put the last layer or two of brick on the top. Of course all we could do to help was carry a few bricks at a time to him. That, of course, made it our wall.

Walls!

It seemed that walls were all we saw of our world. They held us in. They also held out the strangeness of the other world, the outside world.

Our father had tried one day to explain it to us. He said we'd understand it better as we grew older. Ralf

10

and I had often discussed what he had told us, trying to get meaning out of his words.

We here, he said, were fortunate. Our area, like the whole country, had been completely laid waste in the nuclear-radiation war of seventy years before. Most of the cities had no survivors. Here, although the city itself had been destroyed, about one per cent of the population of two million had lived through it.

In struggling up from the great disaster, a few strong leaders had secluded themselves to work out a plan for survival. It was a hard, rigid, tight plan they developed. But it seemed to work.

First rule had been that all offspring of the survivors who showed signs of being affected by the radiation would be killed. The only hope for the race, the new rulers had decreed, was to keep alive only those who were defect-free.

The few pieces of old buildings still standing were pulled down. The whole metropolitan area was then brought to the same level with huge earth-moving equipment saved from the old city. Over the central part of this was laid a thick layer of soil carried in from outside the city. On top of the soil-covered area was built Resurrection City as it now existed.

Each family, after proving it was free of radiation effects, was given a plot of land. Also, because there were still vast quantities of brick and building stone to be disposed of, each family was given a quota for building a home and a high wall around it. Crews erected the homes. The individual head of the family was responsible for using the remainder of his alloted brick for the walls. The more bricks he used on his wall, the more space he had within the wall.

All this our father had tried to explain to us. It seemed to make sense when he told it to us. Afterward, Ralf and I admitted to each other that it was not clear at all.

11

We had made almost the complete circuit of the yard when our father came out of the house and motioned for us to come back in.

Our mother was in the front room, weeping softly. Father, we could see, was equally disturbed but trying not to show his feelings to us.

"The time has come," he said to Ralf as he put his hand on my twin's tousled fair head.

Ralf and I looked at each other a bit bewildered. We had never said goodbye to each other before. Through eyes half filled with tears we merely gazed wonderingly at the other's face.

"One last word, Ralf," our father said. "If you love Rolf, you must never mention to anyone that you have a twin brother. Or if it should slip out accidentally, just say he was your imaginary playmate. Do you promise?"

I saw Ralf nod, unable to say anything.

Then our mother stood up and after throwing her arms around Ralf, took me by the hand and led me down to the basement. There, she led me to the corner where bricks had been piled waiting for later use. She moved a number of them to reveal a small door which she pushed inward. She motioned for me to follow her in.

It was not a large room I entered. It had a narrow cot, a table, and chair that tilted back. There were electric lights. There was even a small viviscreen viewer. One corner had been partitioned off to make a toilet and shower room.

I looked around in dumbfounded amazement. It was a room in our house I didn't know existed. What did it mean? Was I supposed to stay here? I turned to face my mother, but she put her hands in front of her eyes and would not return my questioning gaze.

"Your father will come down, Rolf," she said. "He will explain what all this means."

She paused.

"Just remember, Rolf, that what we do is out of love for you. Your father and I love you very much. Now, just stay here until your father comes to you. Whatever you do, make no sounds and do not leave this room."

II

I was seated on the cot. My father sat opposite me in the chair. He looked unhappy.

"This room," he said to me, "is to be your home from now on."

"But why?" I asked, still not understanding what this room meant or why I should stay here.

Father shook his head sorrowfully. "Take off your shoes," he said.

I obeyed the strange command.

"That is the reason why you must stay here," he said, pointing at my four-toed feet.

I looked at them as if for the first time in my life. It was true that, except for our feet, Ralf and I were identical twins. He had five toes on each foot. I had four. We had often laughed about it. What great difference did it make?

"It's time you knew the facts," my father said gently. "When the city was destroyed in the great war of 1999, all but a few of the people were killed outright. About half of the survivors, it was found, were seriously affected by the nuclear radiation. The other half showed no apparent effects.

"It was decided, if progress was to be made, that no mutants would be allowed to live. I suppose those original leaders felt here, if ever, was a chance to develop a super race. No taints would be permitted. Anyone showing any sign of mutability would be killed.

"As babies were born, they were carefully examined by the city examiner. Those showing defects were done away with. Some mutants fled. Some flawed babies were born and hidden away by their parents . . . just as we are going to try to do for you.

"That, Rolf, is why you are here in this secret room. Six years ago today when you and Ralf were born prematurely, we discovered before the doctor-examiner arrived that you had only four toes on your feet. We knew that as soon as the examiner saw this, you would be taken away and killed. So we didn't tell the doctor-examiner we had a second boy."

"I would have been killed?" I cried in anguish. I looked down at my four-toed feet. "Just because of this?"

"It was enough to brand you as a mutant. Not telling anyone we had two boys was the only way to save you. That's why, in all these years, we have always kept you out of sight when we had visitors or the examiner came."

"So that's why you always hustled us out of the room when anyone came?"

"That's why, Rolf. It was to save you. To your mother and me you are just the same as Ralf. In our eyes you are both fine boys. We couldn't bear to think that you should die simply because you lack a toe on each foot."

"Is it that important—one toe on each foot?"

"The city authorities think it is. To them any sign of abnormality is a deviation from the normal. They seem to be determined that the super race they are developing will have no taint."

"But to be killed because I lack two toes?"

"It's more than that, Rolf. As a mutant, even if you mated with a normal girl, there is high probability that your children would have some kind of taint. If you mated with a mutant girl, it is practically certain your children would be abnormal."

"Abnormal?" I repeated the word. "What does that mean?"

15

Father shook his head. "Some mutants are like you—with only slight defects. But some become monsters—horrible creatures with no arms, with two heads, with huges growths on their bodies, with three or even four legs, beings too hideous to describe."

I shuddered in horror at his words.

"That is why, Rolf, I have built this secret room for you. You have everything here you need. I have hooked in a connection to the pneumatic tube that brings in our food pellets. You merely have to press this button and you can get one any time you are hungry. Water is available in the corner. Over your bed are two lights. When one burns red, you must not leave this room for any reason. When the other burns blue, it is safe for you to come up.

"Starting tomorrow, because our child is no longer here, the rules call for your mother to start working in the central area. Neither of us will be here during the day. If the blue light is burning, you may come up and go outside. If anyone comes to our gate-door, hurry back down to your room as fast as you can. Never let yourself be seen—that is the important thing."

My father stood up and looked around. "It will be hard for you," he sighed. "It will be hard for us. But we'll be happier knowing you are still alive and near us. Mother will see that you get some cooked meals to go with the food pellets. You need vegetables for roughage. And you'll need sunlight and fresh air to keep you well and strong. I have rigged up an air vent to outside to bring you air here, but it is not as good as being outdoors.

"As for entertainment," he went on, "we'll do all we can. The viviscreen may help. We have a few books which mother will try to teach you to read. But remember, your mother and I are just Class Three people. We've had very little education ourselves. Only those with superior promise are given advanced education. We do mechanical work. It is about all we can do. We hope Ralf makes something of himself."

"But me?"I cried. "What chance have I of making anything of myself?"

I started to cry. My father put his arms around me. I could feel the great salty tears splash down from his cheeks onto the back of my neck.

Somehow these tears reassured me. My father loved me. My mother loved me. I was alive because of their love for me. I would do as they asked. But in my heart began the boiling up of hatred for the 'rules and regulations' that made all this necessary. Some day . . . some day those rules would change . . . and some day I would help change them . . .

III

In the lonely days that followed, I tried to keep as active as I could.

Without Ralf to play with, I worked in the garden until there wasn't a single weed left to be pulled, nor a single stalk that had not felt a touch from my caring fingers.

Like all the other Class Three homes, ours had only one floor over a basement. There was a fairly large front room where we ate our meals and spent our evenings together. Off from it was a small kitchen with an electric stove and refrigerator. Behind that was a bathroom. Next to it was a room where mother washed our clothes. In addition there were three bedrooms. Inasmuch as the typical Class Three family had from two to four, or even more children, the three-bedroom arrangement had been made standard.

My parents slept in one room of the bedrooms. The room where Ralf and I had slept was left just as when he departed. The third bedroom was empty.

The walls of the house were of restored brick. Inside, father had plastered them smooth. Mother had covered these smooth white walls with a soft green paint.

Father was an assistant in a laboratory in the center of the city. He never quite made clear to me what 'assisting' work he did. He was not happy in his tasks. To my six-year old eyes, he was big and strong and very handsome. His hair was beginning to turn gray, but he still held himself more erect than most of the men who passed our way. In fact I was always proud to compare him with these men as they moved wearily past the tiny peephole in our front gate-door.

My mother, oddly enough, liked her new work. She said it kept her from thinking about what might be happening to Ralf. Her job, as far as I could figure out, was to help restore objects that had been damaged in the nuclear war. One thing it did—it gave her a chance to save out a few things she thought I might like. These things, books mostly, she would bring home to me, her dark eyes alive with the joy of being able to do something for me. Father said she was too thin. To me, however, she was the most beautiful person in the world, except possibly Elissa.

I tried looking at the books mother brought to me, but there was no way for me to understand them. I looked at the viviscreen. That too palled on me with its steady, droning pounding away at the danger of letting any mutants live.

The one great pleasure I had was to remove the loose bricks in the side wall and peer through unseen at little Elissa.

I studied her by the hour—her carefree ways, her grace, her eagerness for life. I knew it would be worth my life to let her know I was watching her. I was tempted. With Ralf gone, the ache and hunger for a playmate was almost more than I could bear.

One very hot day I was at my secret perch at the side wall when she came out dressed, as usual, in her short white tunic. She started to lie down on the grass, stopped and glanced back toward her house.

I could even hear her giggle as she lifted her tunic over her head. She had nothing on underneath.

Almost as if she knew I was watching and she wanted me to look at her, she lifted her arms overhead and turned slowly, her face raised to the sky, to let the hot sun beat down on all parts of her.

All parts of her! I had never seen a naked girl before. I dared not even blink my eyes for fear she might vanish. Her slenderness. Her soft pink flesh. Her parted

19

lips. Her half closed eyes. Her bare body, so different than Ralf's or mine. Never, in all my life would I ever again see anything so pure, so innocent, so beautiful.

At that instant her mother called to her. With a quick twist of her arms, the tunic was back on and she was heading for the front of her house.

Elissa never again showed herself to me. She played in her yard. She rested there. But the vision I had seen once I never saw again. Possibly the weather grew too cool. Possibly her mother had reprimanded her.

But to me, as I went to sleep each night, in my basement room, the thought I always had before drifting off to sleep was of Elissa, pink and lovely in her nakedness.

With the coming of autumn, there was less for me to do in the garden. I spent long hours peering out through the peephole in the front gate-door. People passed on their way to work or on their way home. They looked tired and unhappy. I realized this was how my father was beginning to look and act, as though something was going out of his spirit. My mother was different. It might have been all for my benefit, but when she came home, she was all smiles, especially when she could bring something for me.

My parents were worried that I was out in the yard as much as I was. They were afraid that somehow— they couldn't say how—someone might see me. I tried to reassure them that I was careful. I even showed them a small shelter I had made for myself out of bricks and had covered with climbing plants. I said I could hide there in an emergency.

Every night, however, I slept in my hidden room. It would be at night, my father said, that the watch guard would come to check any report of an unregistered boy in the house.

I suspected they were afraid Ralf might accidentally speak of a twin brother. It would be easy for a six-year old to forget that he was not to mention my existence. I even overheard my parents, one evening, tell what they would do if the watch guard came. Ralf, they would say, always had a lively imagination. One of his fancies was that he had a twin brother who played with him. Not uncommon a fancy in lonely children. And anyway, come see the bedroom where our dear son Ralf slept alone. It hasn't been touched since he left. Search if you will. You will find no twin boy here.

So they had talked. But I knew they were worried.

People did little visiting around in Resurrection City. Work was hard. Hours were long. There was little time or energy left over, after working and tending one's garden, for socializing.

As cool weather came on, some friends of my parents did drop in occasionally. I was always hustled down to my basement room, there to spend another lonely night.

Then, one evening, the worst possible thing happened. I was in the house waiting for the return of my parents from work. Mother came in first and slumped into a chair. Her face was white. She seemed to be gasping for breath and held a hand clutched to her breast. I stood there helpless, not knowing what to do.

A few minutes later my father came in. He took one look at my mother and rushed over to her. He eased her down as she fell slowly sideways. Frantic with concern, he turned to me. "I must go for a doctor. Stay with her. When you hear me come back, hurry to your basement room. The doctor must not see you."

I nodded that I understood. But it was another thing to stay next to my mother's frail body and see her sinking lower . . . and not be able to help her. I tried talking with her and rubbing her arms and forehead. Once she opened her eyes and a smile came to her lips as she looked at me. Then she went limp again.

When I heard father at the gate-door, I was tempted to stay with my mother in spite of his order to me. I sensed that I might never be able to see her again. What did it matter now if they took me away and killed me because I lacked a toe on each foot?

But then, as though she were giving me a last message of love, I had a feeling that what she would want me to do was to keep on living.

Carefully I let her head fall. One last hug. One last kiss on her lifeless cheek. One last look.

I stood up and headed with stumbling feet for my hidden room.

IV

I turned and tossed all night. My little world had suddenly gone to pieces. First my twin brother had been taken away. Now my sweet and loving mother was dead.

At first I lay on my cot and stared at the red light that burned over my head. Somehow during the night I must have drifted off to sleep. And I dreamed. . . .

I dreamed I was in a large cavern with flames shooting up from openings in the floor and in the side walls. No matter which way I turned, blazing tongues of fire reached out for me. As I crawled frantically on hands and knees through billows of red mist, I could hear cries of pain and terror all around me. I suppose they were my own cries. But to me, in my mad nightmare, I was in a world of horror. Slimy, nauseous creatures slid out of the flames to bar my way. They stretched out their loathsome claws to grab me and pull me into the fires with them.

I woke with a start, my face dripping with hot sweat. My father was shaking my shoulder. "Wake up, Rolf. Wake up. You've had a bad dream."

I looked up. The red light was still burning.

"Yes," my father said, "the red light burns. It would be dangerous for you to come up. There will be people in and out all day. I've slipped away to warn you to stay hidden here until I tell you it is safe for you to come up."

I looked up at my father. His face was contorted with grief for my mother and worry for me. He too was a victim, I realized.

"I hate them," I said between tightly clenched teeth. "They killed my mother."

"No, Rolf. Your mother died of a heart attack. It had nothing to do with you or me or her new work. She would have died anyway."

"They took Ralf away," I muttered. "And now they have killed my mother."

My father shook his head wearily. "Listen, Rolf. Today is a day of great danger for you. There will be people upstairs all day. They must not know you are here. You must stay hidden until they all are gone."

I could see that he was near the breaking point. I tried to reach out to touch his hand. Suddenly he had his arms around me and we were both sobbing.

He broke away and backed up to the small opening that led to the basement. Too emotional to speak, he merely pointed at the red light and crawled through.

I got up slowly, slipped on my wool tunic, and looked around. Ever since Ralf had left, I had slept every night in this room. Suddenly now it took on a new meaning to me. Was this to be my world for the rest of my life? Would the red light keep burning forever? What if my father never came back?

I sat down on the chair. The tears that had come so easily the night before would not come now. I felt drained of feeling.

I knew that I had all the things I needed to survive in this secret room. But did I want to? Was life so precious? Could I face a lifetime here, alone and lonely, for day after day, month after month, year after year?

I had merely to press a button for food pellets. There was water for drinking and bathing. Several changes of clothing were on hooks on the wall, even larger sizes for me to grow into.

But how could I use my time? I had books I couldn't read. I had a viviscreen that I hated. I had a few games mother had shown me how to play with, but most required a partner.

And always there would be the red light. The red

light of warning. The red light of nightmares, of horrible creatures that grabbed at me. Always there would be the red light of danger . . .

A sobbing shook me. No tears came, only a deep convulsive sobbing that tore at me and left me weak.

What I did the rest of that day I have no recollection. I must have done something for it did pass.

A clock was part of my viviscreen. Father had taught me to tell time. I could tell that it was evening because a small black panel showed. If it were morning, the panel would be white. The hands on the clock told me that it was only an hour before midnight.

As it had been all day, the red light was still burning . . .

Suddenly I saw it switch off and then come back on again. An instant later, the blue light came on. This was something that had never happened before—both lights on at the same time.

Had someone discovered the light switches upstairs, a stranger who didn't know what they were for? Terror seized me. Where was my father? Why had he not come down again? Had he been taken away? Was I to be left alone here?

Then, I knew I wanted to live. I had to live. For more than six years my mother and father had risked their own lives by keeping me hidden and alive. I crept over to the hole in the wall through which I had to go to .ach the basement of our house. I removed two of the loose bricks. I listened.

At first I could hear nothing. Then came the sound of talk from upstairs. It was not my father's voice.

Pulling a few more of the bricks away, I looked out. Only one dim light was on over the bottom of the stairway going to the upper floor. There was no one in the asement. Carefully I removed the rest of the bricks 1 wormed my way out.

At the stairs I hesitated. What I was doing was

exactly what my father had told me not to do. But I had to know what was happening. Holding the hand rail I moved up the stairs one by one, testing each step to avoid even the slightest sound. My heart was pounding.

At the top of the stairs I halted again. The room ahead was the kitchen. It was dark. Taking a tentative step in, I saw instantly there were several men in the front room. I pulled back and watched and listened.

My father was seated. In front of him was a man in the uniform of the watch guard. The man was reading from a paper. I could not hear all that was being read to my father, only a word now and then. My father merely sat quietly listening, his eyes downcast, his face expressionless.

By moving a bit to my left, I could see there were two other men in the room, both dressed in watch guard uniforms. They were informing father of something, probably more of those 'rules and regulations' that filled several of the books mother had been able to get for me. I sensed, from the look on his face, that my father found the words unwelcome.

When the reading was over, I saw my father stand up and reach out for the paper. The officer passed it over to him. The three uniformed men turned to go.

I dodged back out of sight and scurried down the stairs, across to the entrance to my hidden room. There I quickly arranged the bricks and crawled back in. I looked at the signal lights—both were still burning.

For half an hour I sat, my legs trembling under me, my heart beating a wild race with itself. Finally I heard a sound in the basement beyond. Bricks were being moved. Strangely I felt no fear. It was too late for fear. I listened and waited. Faintly I could hear the sound of heavy boots. Some of the bricks shielding the entrance were moved and then dropped. The men were making a search. Had someone told them of an unregistered boy? Had father, somehow, revealed my presence? But no, if that had happened, they would have known where to look. And I had great faith that my father would never tell.

For another hour I waited in silence. And always over my cot were the red and blue lights still burning. Remembering that I had eaten nothing since noontime, I was about to press the button that would give me a food pellet. Then I remembered it was connected with the main supply tube to our house. There might be a click that would alert the men upstairs. I found some raw carrots and chewed on them.

Another hour passed. Then, without warning, there was a sound in the basement beyond my room. A moment later my father came through the opening.

"I'm sorry, father," I said. "I went up. I saw the men talking to you."

"Yes, Rolf, those men were here to tell me what I had to do now that your mother is dead."

I pointed at the red and blue lights still on. "I was worried when they both came on."

"One of the men saw the switches and tried them. Afterward I didn't dare go back and check which lights were on."

"They came into the basement."

"Yes, they decided to make a thorough search of the house while they were here. I was very frightened when I saw one of the men start to move some of the bricks that hid the opening to your room. I explained they were some I planned to use to make another layer on top of our wall."

He sat down on my cot and took his head in his hands. He stared unseeing at the floor. "And now," he said in a voice so low I could hardly hear him, ". . . and now I have a new problem."

He looked up at me. "There is a rule that when either a man or a woman dies, the survivor has two choices. He can move into a central dormitory with

27

other single people. Or, if he wants to keep his home, he must take on a new mate."

I looked at him with surprise.

"Yes, Rolf, either I have to leave this house which would bring instant exposure for you. Or I must accept another woman as my new mate. Nor is that a sure solution. It would have to be a Class Three woman and all Class Three people are trained to fear and hate mutants. There is almost no chance that I could find a new mate who would be willing to help hide you. She would not have your mother's love for you. Knowing how they keep pounding away at the evils of mutations, it is extremely unlikely I would get a mate who would be willing to risk her life as your mother did for you."

He sighed in despair.

I put my hand on his shoulder. "Is there any way I could leave the city? Go away?"

He looked up. "Go out of the city? It is impossible. No one can go beyond the walls of the city. No one has for over half a century. There is only wilderness out there—wild beasts, and worse, wild people, offspring of mutants who managed to escape the city in those early years. No, there is no hope there. I see no hope anywhere."

He stood up to leave. "There is only one good thing. I do not have to choose a new mate right away. If I go to the central dormitory, I could go any time. If I agree to take another mate, the authorities will give me time to make my choice. There are more single women than men. I will be permitted to interview several. My only hope is that I can find one I can persuade to help shield you as your mother did."

Saying this, he almost seemed anxious to hurry out. It was as though he couldn't face me any longer . . . as though he felt he was failing me.

A few minutes later, as I got into bed, I glanced up at the lights. Now, only the red light was burning.

V

I saw little of my father in the dismal days that followed. Of course there wasn't much he could do for me. I had food and water. For the time being, at least, I was safe.

I had a few weeks, I hoped, before father's new mate would be coming. What would she be like? Would she accept me as a son? From father's expression, I sensed that this was not likely to happen.

A few weeks . . . a month or two . . . and then what?

Try to leave the city? I had never been beyond the wall that surrounded our yard. I would have no idea where to go.

During the early autumn days I spent a great deal of time in the garden, pulling up the last of the vegetables before frost set in. It was pleasant to put my fingers into the ground still warm and moist from the fall rains.

Also I spent many hours peering through my secret opening in the side wall, hoping to catch glimpses of Elissa in the yard next door. I saw her at times, usually bundled up against the cooling weather. She seemed less carefree and happy than before. Her play was quiet and subdued as though the intense joy of living had left her.

One terrible day I guessed why. Elissa was approaching her sixth birthday, and she was dreading it as Ralf and I had dreaded it.

I spent most of my time in the next few days waiting and looking. Then it happened. I had just pulled the loose bricks away when I saw Elissa and her parents standing rigidly at the front of their house. Before them was a watch guard officer.

I heard Elissa let out a cry of despair and then throw

herself into her mother's arms. Her father put his arms around her and gently pulled her away and into the hands of the officer.

The last I saw of Elissa was her heavy outer tunic shaking with sobs as the officer led her away. Numbly, I put the bricks back into their place. Later I would mix up some mortar and fix them permanently into position.

Somehow this was a different kind of loss than when Ralf was taken away and my mother died. This made me angry. I went to our front gate-door and peeked out. In the next hour a dozen or more people passed. They shuffled along, eyes downcast, their shoulders hunched over. Was this what life was all about? Was this all anyone had to look forward to in Resurrection City?

I went back into the house and down into my basement room. I turned on the viviscreen. As always I found I hated it—the everlasting tirade against mutants! All it seemed to say was that mutants must be killed on sight. No mutant must be allowed to taint the 'pure' strain of the new super race. Mutants were evil and loathsome and did unspeakable crimes.

I thought to myself—I am a mutant and I am not loathsome, nor have I done any unspeakable crimes. I turned off the receiver.

In the sudden stillness, I heard a new sound. I listened. Finally I got to my knees and put an ear to the floor.

There was a strange pounding sound below. It was very faint. But it was unmistakable that someone was below my room. For an hour it went on. Then it stopped and did not resume.

That evening my father came again. He said that visitors had stopped coming, but it would be best for me to continue staying in my room at night. I didn't tell him about seeing Elissa being taken away. Ralf and I had never told our parents about her, or even about the break in the wall. It was our big secret. I did, however, tell him about hearing faint sounds of pounding below my floor. He looked startled.

"Rolf," he said, "there is great danger in the area below us."

"Danger . . . what kind of danger?"

"I have never told you because I thought you were safe here and it would only frighten you to know."

"Know what, father?"

"When the war ended just before the end of the century, remember how I told you the city was destroyed and only a few people survived—not more than one out of a hundred. Half of them were affected by the radiation. Those that had mutant children were put to death. Some escaped and burrowed down into the ruins of the old city which covered an area five or six times as large as our new city. That's where they live—thousands of them now, I understand."

"An underground city below us?" I asked in surprise. "Right under us here?"

"Probably not directly under us. I have been told they have not done much burrowing under the new city. Too difficult."

"Is that what I heard? What if they came up? What should I do?"

My father put a comforting hand on my arm. "So far they have had a hard enough time to survive. I don't think they'll come up here."

"What was the pounding for?"

"I really don't know. I can only guess. I hear rumors that even after seventy years, the city authorities have not found a way to go very deep into the lower city and capture the mutants there. Our watch guard is made up entirely of Class Two men. It is really a very small organization. Hardly enough men to protect the central area and the food storehouses. Perhaps the mutants below are having their troubles too and are probing the ruins to find new materials they can use."

I thought for a moment. "Father, would it be possible for me to go into the underground and join the mutants? After all, I am a mutant too."

He turned his face away before answering. "Yes, I suppose it is possible. But I don't advise it."

"Why? Wouldn't I then be among my own kind?"

Father shook his head sadly. "I know that much of what we are told about mutants over the viviscreen are lies. All I know is that I know very little that is truth about them. We know nothing of how they live. Every once in awhile one is captured and put to death. I have seen viviscreen showings of some of these poor creatures —horrible monstrosities, misshapen and hideous. No, Rolf, stay here in your room as long as you can. Maybe we'll be able to think of something."

"When do you have to choose your new mate, father?"

"That's my last hope, Rolf. Next week I am to meet three women the authorities have chosen for me to interview. I will try to sound out each of them on how she feels about mutants. I have to be careful. If I show real sympathy for them, they could report me. They would end all our hopes. For the same reason it is going to be difficult to get one of these women to admit she feels sympathy for them. No one dares speak his true thoughts."

For several days I listened whenever I could with my ear to the floor. The pounding sound was never repeated.

But the thought remained. If there was a world of mutants in the lower city, why shouldn't I join them? Perhaps father's fears were groundless. Perhaps the underworld people were eager to accept mutants escaping from the upper world. After all, that's where they all came from originally. Perhaps I would find a family to join ... even other children to play with.

One night my father came to me again. He remarked how pale I was getting. With no garden to work in, no Elissa to watch, I had little desire to wander around the cold, winter-struck yard.

That was the night he told me about the three women.

One, he said, was young and quite pretty. She would have brightened up the home he was sure. But when he brought up the subject of mutants, she became bitter and hateful in her denunciation of them. Her indoctrination on the subject had been thorough and complete.

The second woman was about his own age, but expressed no interest in having him select her. She had had a mate who died. She wanted no new mate.

The third one was slightly older than father but still well within the child bearing age. She had been mated once before when she was much younger. When her child was born, it was found to be a mutant. Both she and her mate were rechecked and it was found that the father was the tainted party. The man and child were put to death. She had told him this when he first mentioned mutants. From her expression, he could see that she was the most bitter of all the women in her hatred of mutancy.

"Then there is no hope?" I asked.

"There is always hope," my father murmured. "I can report to the authorities that the second woman does not want to mate again. I can ask for a substitute."

The next day I spent some time thinking of what father had said about the women. I could see little hope there. If he failed with the substitute, what choice did I have but to try to get into the underground city? I had little to lose by going there. I would see what was below my floor.

Just the thought of having a project to be working on gave me new heart. I got out the digging tools we used

33

in our garden. I carefully marked off a place in the corner where I would start.

I was smiling when I made the first strike with the pick.

VI

Sometimes it seemed as if I made no progress at all after hours of hard pounding and prying and shoveling. Each day, I took the debris up to the back yard and buried it.

The days, now filled with work, slipped rapidly by . . .

I knew I was digging down into a mass of strange material. At the top it was mostly just soil and loose stone. As I went lower I found I was entering layers of slabs and blocks which were lying in confused disorder. When I couldn't move an obstacle, I went around it, as I had to do often when I came to portions of steel girders.

About every third evening my father came down to see what I had accomplished. After a first effort to discourage me, he said no more against my digging. For one thing he said he could see the exercise was doing me good.

He explained the steel girders by saying the old city had used them extensively in the frameworks of buildings twenty, fifty, even a hundred stories high. The nuclear blasts had toppled them all over. After the war, huge tractor-dozers were used to level the whole area.

What I would find in the space below our house he said he could not imagine. He had no knowledge of what had stood there before. He did believe, however, that the leveling off process had resulted in a thick layer of rubble below us. It could be as much as six or seven times the height of our house.

"And the mutants live there?" I asked.

"From what I know, there are a lot of them down there. Several thousand probably. I don't believe they occupy the space directly below us. More likely they do their burrowing away from where Resurrection City was built, but still within the limits of the old city."

"How do they live?"

My father laughed at this question. "From the way you've been digging, you are likely to find out before I do."

"You're not going to stop me?"

"No, Rolf. I feel I have failed you. I have found no woman to mate with that has sympathy for mutants. All I can do now is choose one that would be least likely to go snooping around the basement. That way I can keep the house and you might be able to stay in your room a little longer."

"When do you have to choose?"

"Soon." He looked at me sadly. "I only wish you were older. You are so young to be going down to live with the mutants."

"If I do find a way to go down, what should I do?"

"I wouldn't know, Rolf. I wouldn't know what to do myself. But I've been thinking about it, knowing you could be breaking through any day now. Tonight I have brought you several items which might be useful. I confess I had to steal them from a storeroom."

He opened a cloth bag and spilled a number of items out on the cot. He pointed to them.

"Here is an electric torch with a dozen spare batteries. This is a plastic water bottle. This is a hand axe with a sharp, hardened blade. Here is a compass. On the surface it always points north. Down below, with all those steel girders, I'm not sure where it will point.

"And here is a laser hand gun, one of the many thousands left over from the war of 1999. All the watch guards carry them. I stole this one, but was able to get only a half dozen extra charges. Use it only to protect your own life. At full power it will burn a hole in a piece of steel or in a man. Here, I'll show you how to aim it and where to activate it so the beam can be directed at your target."

I looked down at the various items. Up until now, the digging had been not much more than something for me to do. Now, with these tools, escape to the underworld not only seemed possible, it seemed that nothing could stop me.

Actually it took another two weeks before I reached what looked like a crude passageway in the debris. At least I could see signs that someone had pounded and pried metal beams to allow passage room.

I had been using a light from my room on an extension cord to show where to dig. That cord had reached its limit. I knew the time had come for me to make my final step and explore the passage I had discovered.

I went back to my room. For more than two days I stayed in the room, hoping my father would come. I wanted desperately to say goodbye to him. Throughout this period the red light kept burning. After making such fine progress in my digging, I didn't want to get caught now. On the third day of waiting, I heard sounds at my entrance hole.

It was father. He had a frightened look on his face.

"I can only stay a minute," he whispered. "They insisted I choose one of the women today. It was that or lose the house. She is upstairs now. It's the substitute I asked for, and I really know very little about her."

He looked down into the hole I had dug. "How much longer will it take?"

"I can go now," I said. "I've been waiting to say goodbye to you."

We looked at each other, pain in our expressions.

"I'll try to keep the room hidden," he said. "If you need me, just come back to the room. I'll try to check here as often as I can."

We embraced as only a father and a son can. Again, as on my sixth birthday, I felt his hot tears on the back of my neck. I was coming back, I knew I would. I'll be seeing him again. Maybe I could even find a way to get him out too. We'd go together. Perhaps even to beyond the high walls of the city. Maybe it was better out there than he thought. It couldn't be much worse than here.

When he left, I could hear him piling the bricks higher than ever in front of the opening to my room.

I took a bath and put on my warmest and best tunic, my best footwear. Quickly I filled the cloth bag with the things I wanted to take with me—the laser gun, the hatchet, the electric torch, enough food pellets for a month, and the water bottle.

Then, taking a last look around, I turned off all the lights, leaving only the red light still burning. With the cloth bag hung over my shoulder in a sling arrangement, I started my descent into the unknown world below Resurrection City.

VII

I descended slowly and carefully through the well-like hole I had made through the tangled mass of materials. There were great blocks of concrete and stone. There were squares of hard tile. There were large pieces of metal. There were strips of artificial wood paneling, most of it fused together but some of it still showing the beauty of its original graining.

I wondered if the whole area under Resurrection City was made up of these jumbled-up scraps of building materials. Why had not the survivors of the war made use of them? Why had they covered all this over?

When I reached the level where I had found what I believed to be a man-made passageway, I had to decide which way to go, left or right. I chose right.

Before I left the spot, however, I marked it with a crayon on the side of a slab of stone. Looking upwards at the hole I had created, I could see that no one would be able to identify it as an escape route to the top. And yet I knew I might have to use it in an emergency.

In an emergency? Everything was an emergency from now on. I was headed into a land as alien to me as if I were suddenly plunked down into the middle of the Class One rulers' headquarters. In fact in this strange place, I was the alien.

For an hour I moved step by step, never taking more than a half stride at a time. Every two or three minutes I would stop, turn off my electric torch, and listen.

If what father had told me about the mutants was only half true, I wanted to have as much warning as possible when I did stumble onto them.

As I moved through the tangled mass, I could see that

whatever leveling off had been done had not really compressed the various materials. They were loose, with great air pockets. It explained why the air was quite breathable.

At times, too, I saw that efforts had been made to cut back into the mass where it was less dense. I explored several of these side tunnels only to find them blind alleys.

Once, when I was resting with the light off, I was nearly startled out of my wits by a strange sound ahead. I held my breath in terror. Stealthily I slipped the laser gun out of my bag. In my other hand I held my electric torch without putting it on. I waited. I listened. The minutes slipped by tortuously. Cool as it was in this underground world, I could feel the sweat of fear come to my forehead.

Then I heard it again . . .

Quickly I snapped on my light. The beam shot out in front of me. At first, half blinded myself by the sudden return of light, I could see nothing. Then I saw it—two gleaming yellow-green spots of light reflecting the glare of my torch.

A cat! It had to be a cat. Although I had never seen one before, I knew what they looked like from pictures. It just crouched in the passageway ahead of me and stared at me as though questioning my right to intrude on its domain. Gradually I drew air into my lungs, almost with a sigh of relief.

A cat then was to be my first contact with the denizens of the vast, mysterious world below Resurrection City. I moved a step toward the furry animal. It turned and moved back out of sight. I followed. Around the first turn in the twisting path I saw the cat waiting for me. When I came into its sight, again it moved away.

For half an hour I followed the small creature. In some ways it brought waves of fear to me to be pursuing this silent, slinking beast. And yet, back in my mind was the hope that it would lead me to its master, or at least other human beings. I knew I had to make contact with the mutants sooner or later.

A thought came to me. Was it possible that the cat was deliberately leading me into a trap? Well, if so, at least it was a trap I was entering of my own free will. After all, the basement room was a trap too. The danger there was real and certain. Here it was unreal and uncertain.

The cat disappeared. For some time I waited for it to come back. If its purpose had been to lure me into some unearthly dangers, it had apparently given up. Or perhaps it had been merely curious about me.

I directed the beam of my torch around. It was not too hard to guess that where I was standing had once been a building with rooms and hallways. Portions of the collapsed walls still held firm. There was even a half open door.

Passing through the doorway, I could see a rubble-filled room with what looked like chairs and tables and even the metal skeleton of a bed. Most of the items were piled in one corner, smashed almost beyond recognition. The bed, however, held its shape. It had a metal frame with metal springs. It was tipped on one side but I found it easy to bring it upright again.

After the tension of my slow crawl through the ruins, I was weary. The metal bed, hard as it was, was at least level, and it did look inviting. Before going on, it would be well for me to get some sleep. A few hours of rest would be welcome.

I took a drink from my bottle of water and chewed on a food pellet. Then, after using my bag of supplies as a pillow, I crawled over on the bed and tried to go to sleep. It was difficult. My mind kept returning to my father and mother and Ralf, and then to Elissa. Had I made a mistake in leaving the basement room? Was I safe in this unnatural cave, with the rubble of a ruined city crowding down on top of me?

In spite of myself, I started to sob softly to myself. Even the long, lonely days and nights in my hidden room were not like this. There, at least I had solid walls around me. And I had father only a floor above me, to shield me from the terrors of the night.

Here, I felt utterly alone and deserted. It was not just the darkness. It was darkness bred of despair, an overwhelming pushing down of oppressive darkness that drained me of all courage . . . even of hope.

I must have slept . . .

When I awoke, I was startled by the intense dark. It must always be dark in these ruins, I reasoned with myself as I struggled up from my deep sleep. I reached around for the electric torch in my bag. The bag was not under my head. I stretched out my hands to search for it.

It was gone!

I gritted my teeth to hold back a sob. I was alone in the dark—no torch, no gun, no food pellets, no water.

I lay motionless, trying to get control of myself. Of all the things that could happen to me, this was the worst. I slipped my legs over the edge of the metal bed. Again I moved my hands around as far as I could reach. My hope was that the bag had merely fallen off the bed and was on the littered floor.

I remembered there had been a chair on its side about three steps from the bed. I shuffled blindly toward where I thought it was.

Strange! The chair was upright. I let my hand slide across the arm rest. I was just about to move around to the front of the chair when suddenly, without sound or warning, my arm was seized in a tight grip. I let out an only half-muffled shriek of terror. . . .

VIII

"Who are you, boy? Where do you come from? Why are you here?" The voice was low but firm.

Still shaking from shock, I had difficulty finding any words to reply.

"Could I have a light?" I asked weakly.

There was a moment of silence, then a soft laugh. "Afraid of the dark, eh?"

The grasp on my arm was released. A feeble light sprang up, a candle. I looked at the person who sat in the chair facing me. He was a man past middle age, older than my father. His face was gaunt. Dark eyes probed at me. A fringe of white hair rimmed his bald scalp. His eyebrows, however, were long and dark and bushy. He was smiling.

Then I noticed, lying on his lap, was the cat I had seen the night before. I pointed. "Is that yours?"

He ran his hand along the fur on its back. It purred with delight. Somehow the sight of the gentle motion gave me a small measure of reassurance.

"This is Witch, my close friend," the man said.

"A real witch?" I asked tremulously, not quite sure I knew what a witch was or how I should treat it.

"Before I answer any of your questions, boy, you'll have to answer mine. To start off—where do you come from?"

I pointed up.

"Oh, a boy from Resurrection City! Don't you know this place is dangerous for Resurrection boys? Down here in Destruction City, they kill Resurrection people on sight just as they kill us on sight up there. How did you get here?"

43

"I crawled down through a hole and then followed an opening in the ruins." I peered hopefully at him. "Are you a mutant?" I asked.

The man laughed. "No, I'm not a mutant, at least not a disfigured one. Not all of us in Destruction City are what you would call mutants."

"Do you hate and fear them?" I asked.

"Hate them? No, why should I? Sometimes I fear them—the more violent ones. But most of them are gentle and kind. No, I don't hate them."

"Then you wouldn't hate me if I told you I was a mutant? You wouldn't kill me?"

Again the man laughed, a low, soft chuckle. "No, I wouldn't hate you, nor would I kill you."

He reached around and pulled out my bag of supplies from the other side of the chair. The cat jumped gracefully off the man's lap and came sidling up to me, rubbing its silken body against my leg.

"Witch likes you," he said as he handed me my bag. "You'd better have a food pellet and some water."

I offered him one of the pellets, but he refused with a smile. While I ate, he kept watching me intently. At the same time I had a chance to study him too.

There was a wise goodness shining in his expression. Even his scanty white hair framed a face that was strong and yet gentle. I had the feeling that if he were to stand up, he would be very tall and commanding in appearance.

I could not resist the question—"If you are not a mutant, why are you here?"

His expression changed as bitterness filled it. "Resurrection City is an abomination," he exclaimed almost angrily. Then he forced himself to smile. "It's a long story. But now, my boy, tell me about yourself. If you are truly a mutant, how were you able to live up there? Explain that."

I searched for the right words. "I am alive because

44

my father and mother shielded me. They built a hidden room in the basement of our house and I have been living there."

"Why did you leave?"

"My mother died. To keep the house my father had to take a new mate. We both were afraid she would discover my hiding place and tell the authorities. That's why I left."

"In what way are you a mutant?"

For answer I pulled off one shoe and showed him my four-toed foot.

"Yes," he agreed, "according to the unjust laws of Resurrection City, that brands you as a mutant. What a pity." He shook his head in sympathy. "So you came down here to be among other mutants?"

"My father said I would be killed by the watch guard if they found out about me. He didn't know what would happen to me here. He didn't want me to come. But he didn't stop me either."

The man kept looking at me quizzically as though trying to make up his mind what he should do about me.

"What is your name?" he asked.

"Rolf."

"How old are you?"

"More than six, but less than seven."

"Have you any idea what life is like here among the mutants of Destruction City?"

I shook my head.

"Have you learned to read and write?"

Again I shook my head, but added, "I know a little. My mother showed me what the alphabet characters are. That's all."

"Would you like to learn to read and write?"

I nodded eagerly.

He began to rub his hand across the back of the cat. He spoke in a soft voice, almost as though he were just talking to himself.

"Perhaps this is it," he mused. "Perhaps your coming is what I have been waiting for." He peered over at me. "Are you afraid of me?"

"No," I murmered in reply. "I don't think so."

"Are you afraid of the dark?"

"Sometimes."

"Would you be afraid if I put out the candle and I talked to you in the dark?"

"Not as long as you stayed with me."

"All right, Rolf. Hand me the candle and I'll put it out. Then I'll tell you who I am, and the plan that is only now beginning to form in my mind. I know that you are very young and may not understand all that I am going to tell you. But, if you are to do what I'd like you to do, you'll have to know."

I handed him the candle. He blew out the flame. Tiny as it had been, it was still all the light we had. As darkness crushed down on me, I felt again its awful weight— deadening and terrifying.

"My name is Milo," he said. "Thirty years ago I was a Class Three citizen in Resurrection City. I had a mate, a beautiful woman with long, dark hair, gentle and loving. We had a child. It was born with a bit of webbing between its fingers. A doctor's knife would have corrected the flaw in two minutes. But no—the doctor reported the baby's defect. Waiting for the watch guard to come to take the baby away to be killed and to take us in for a genetic check, I knew one or both of us would be accused of carrying the mutant strain and would die.

"In that hour while we were waiting with our baby for the watch guard to come, I decided not to accept this fate. I picked up the baby and told my mate to follow me. Thirty years ago it was easier to get down into the underground city. I had heard stories of openings that led below.

"I took as many food pellets with me as I could

carry. My mate was so weak from the child-bearing she could hardly walk. I took her to the old part of the city where no soil had been used to cover the ruins.

"It was there I searched for and found an opening leading to a narrow tunnel going down. I was challenged by mutant guards at several points. My story was accepted, with the help of my food pellets. We reached the lower city.

"It seems so long ago. It's even hard for me to remember what my mate and I had to do to convince the leaders of the mutants that we be permitted to stay. But we did.

"They sent us to a new marginal area in the underground that was just being explored. They told us we would have to provide for ourselves. The water supply was no problem. They had tapped an underground main. Food, however, we would have to find for ourselves. I soon discovered that there was only one way to get food—steal it from the upper level!

"The food pellets I had brought lasted us for nearly two months. The baby, sadly, died within the first month. Within another month my mate died, partly the result of our flight right after the birth of our child, and partly through grief at losing it.

"I was now alone. That was when I decided I would do everything I could to help the poor, starving mutants in the lower city. And too, I was filled then with the feeling of vengeance against the cruel rulers of the upper city.

"I developed schemes for sorties above. We raided storehouses. We kept harassing the watch guard. We even killed a few.

"Then one day something happened to me. It happens often in this great heap of rubble. I was climbing up one of the exit openings we had made to the surface and fell. I received a broken hip. Without proper medical attention, it left me crippled for life. I can move slowly on a level plane. But I cannot climb any more.

"That's when my hope to get revenge ended. Oddly enough, with the crippling, the urge for revenge faded away. I had then only one aim left—an intense desire to help the mutants.

"I came into this relatively unexplored and undeveloped part of the ruins and established myself here. I became, I suppose, a kind of combination teacher-and-counselor to all who need help. Food was brought to me and what other few things I needed.

"I have a collection of several thousand books saved from the old city. I have taught, crudely perhaps, at least half of the mutant children how to read and write. As I should like to teach you, Rolf.

"And now, my boy, I come to the reason why I have told you this long story about myself. You can guess, can't you?"

For a moment I wasn't sure he really meant for me to reply. Then his hand reached out in the dark and took my arm.

"I am growing old, Rolf. That's why I am telling you all this. I need to train someone to take my place when I die."

"But I'm not even seven years old," I said falteringly.

"All the better," he said with that low chuckle of his. "I believe I can live another dozen years. You will then be eighteen—old enough to be the new teacher-leader."

"How can I be a leader? I know nothing of things here."

"You'll learn. I'll teach you."

There was a sudden burst of flame and the candle was lit. I rubbed my eyes. The man who called himself Milo was smiling.

Again he handed me my bag of supplies. "It could be death for you to wander into Destruction City alone and weaponless. Yes, I know you have a laser gun. You saw how easily I took it from you. Don't count on weapons. The mutants would tear you apart if they found you now. Instead I want you to go back to your basement room."

"But my father's new mate—she will report me!"

"Not if your father tells her he will throw her down among the mutants if she does. It is a threat that would scare any woman."

I shivered with dread at the thought. "But if I go to my room, how will I get to learn how to read and write?"

"That, Rolf, is the other part of my plan. For two days every week, you will leave your room and come down and stay with me in this secluded part of Destruction City. I will teach you on these two days. You'll study the books I give you to take back to your room. By the time you are eighteen, you will be ready to take my place.

"And, Rolf, don't ever forget that you yourself are a mutant. These people here would kill you now before you could even show them your four-toed feet. Later they will hail you as their saviour.

"That's all I will say now, Rolf. Go back up. Talk to your father. Help him persuade his new mate to help you. Then return here in five days."

I nodded numbly. It was almost too much for me to understand. But I would try. I would try.

IX

In my room I found all just as I had left it. I had been
gone only a day and yet it seemed an eternity.

The red light was burning so I knew I would have to
wait for my father to come to me. The question in my
mind was how soon would he come? He had no way
of knowing that I had returned so soon. It might be
days before he had the chance to slip down to see if I
had come back.

Knowing my father, I felt he would be looking in on
my room very quickly, possibly that same day. I was
right. That evening I heard sounds of bricks being
moved. A moment later my father's smiling face appeared in the opening.

From the way he hugged and kissed me, one would
imagine I had been gone for months. Finally he sat
down on the cot, with me next to him.

"What happened, Rolf? Did you get down . . .
below?"

"Yes, father. I went down and spent the night there."

"The mutants—did they accept you?"

"I saw no mutants. But I know more about them now.
I think there is hope for me."

He took my hand in his and pressed it warmly. "Tell
me all about it."

"As you said, father, our city has been built on top
of a thick layer of rubble. Down there where the mutants
live, they call it Destruction City."

"How did you find that out?"

"Well, father, after I climbed down, I set off very
slowly along the narrow, twisting passageway I had
found earlier. Whoever made the passage had to move

great piles of broken and crushed building materials. Even steel girders. I went very carefully. That's when I saw the cat."

"A cat? You saw a cat? Did it attack you?"

"No, it sort of led me on. I came to a hollow space in the ruins. I saw an old metal bed. I was tired. I went to sleep."

"Was the cat still with you?"

"No. It had disappeared before I found the room."

"What happened then?"

"In the morning, when I awoke, I found my bag of supplies gone. Even the electric torch. I could see nothing. I reached around trying to find the bag when my arm was grabbed. There was a man there. He lit a candle and I saw him. He was older than you, father. He had a fringe of white hair around the edge of his head. And heavy dark eyebrows. And dark, piercing eyes. The cat was on his lap. He said his name was Milo. He also said he was not a mutant."

"How can that be, Rolf? I thought there were only mutants in the lower city."

"He and his mate had a mutant baby and he took them there thirty years ago. They are dead, but he still stays. He is crippled. He says all he wants to do now is help the mutants. He even has a plan to help me."

"A plan? What kind of plan?"

"He says it is too dangerous right now for me to join the mutants in Destruction City. He wants me to continue to stay here in my hidden room. Two days every week he wants me to come down and stay with him. He's going to teach me to read and write."

"Stay here the rest of the time?" my father explained. "Didn't you tell him that I have a new mate who probably would report you the first time she learns you are here?"

"I told him that. He said you should threaten to throw her down to the mutants if she told."

Father stared at me. After a shocked first minute or so, he started to laugh. "Yes, it just might work." His brow wrinkled with thought. "Perhaps I have an even better argument. My new mate likes it in our house very much. She has been living with the other unmated women in the women's dormitory. Yes, she likes her independence here very much. Also she wants a child. Only I can give her a child. She is a good worker, a good housekeeper, a good woman. But she is quite homely. She knows I am her last and only chance to have a mate. Especially one who can give her a baby. I think if I tell her about you and that only by helping me hide you can she have me as a mate, my home to live in, and a child. I can save the threat of tossing her to the mutants as a last resort. Of course you know I wouldn't do that to her. It makes a good threat though."

He stood up, his face set with determination. "I'll talk to her right now."

He started toward the opening, then stopped and turned. "Watch the lights. If both the red and blue lights go on, leave at once. Go back to your friend below. It will mean I have failed. If the red light burns steady, merely stay here until I come to you. If the blue light goes on, it means I have talked to her and you are to come up."

"What is her name?"

"It's Gretta. Really she is a very nice person. Not very attractive, but pleasant. I hope her indoctrination has not spoiled her for listening to reason. Of course she is not like your own mother."

With that he left. I heard the concealing bricks being replaced.

For several minutes I merely stared at the red light. Then I realized nothing could happen this soon. My father would have to take his time, sound her out, and approach the subject with caution and care.

I sat on the cot and thought of my mother. How sweet

and pretty she had been. How loving and thoughtful. And then, because I was sad and my heart was heavy, I thought too of little Elissa. What was happening to her? She would be taking the regular training courses. Lastly I thought of Ralf, my twin brother. How I missed him. How good it would have been to have him with me on my trip to the underworld of mutants. Ralf— where was he now? Possibly he and Elissa were in the same classes together. Before I was quite aware of it, I found my head buried in my hands and I was shaking with deep, convulsive sobs.

Finally I wiped my eyes and glanced at the lights . . . The blue light was shining bright and alone!

Had father really succeeded?

I hurried to the water tap and rinsed my face with cold water. With my fingers I flattened my hair into a semblance of order. A moment later I was crawling out of my room. No one was in the basement. I moved cautiously to the bottom of the stairs. I could hear no sounds from above.

Out of long habit I climbed the stairs making as little noise as I could. At the top I glanced quickly into the kitchen. No one was there either. I peered around into the front room. I could see father sitting stiffly on a chair. His new mate was not in my range of vision.

"Come on in, Rolf," my father called out. "We are waiting for you."

I know my lips were trembling and my knees shaking as I took a deep breath and stepped forward.

X

My father's new mate was sitting in a chair opposite him. As father had said, she was not young and pretty like my mother. But there was warmth in her smile as she stood up to greet me.

"Why, he's a beautiful boy!" she exclaimed. Then, without saying another word, she put her arms around me and hugged me as my mother used to. Never had I felt so relieved. The tensions of the past day or two slipped away as though they had never been. The tears when they came were tears of a new kind of happiness. I felt now I had a new mother.

I could see that father was very happy too.

After the first few minutes, Gretta, my new mother, insisted on getting something cooked for me to eat. "Those food pellets are all right for grown ups," she said. "But a growing boy needs fresh natural foods."

After I had eaten, we discussed what we should do. It was agreed that I should continue to sleep in the hidden room. The watch guard had the privilege of making unscheduled visits to Class Three houses at any time. They usually came, however, at night.

My father said he felt it was reasonably safe for me to come out into the yard during the daytime. It was still winter, but spring was not too far off. Gretta was pleased to hear that I did much of the gardening. She said, being unmated, she had lived in the dormitory and had never had a garden of her own to work in. She would be glad to have my help.

I made it clear how important it was for me to spend two days a week with my new friend, Milo.

Gretta asked—"How is it possible for you to go down

there? You said yourself the mutants would probably kill you if they found you came from the upper city."

I tried to answer her with the little information I had. "As I understand it, Resurrection City is on top of only a small portion of the old ruined city. Because of the soil that was put over the rubble in this limited area, air does not filter down. So there are no mutants directly below us."

"I'm glad to hear that," Gretta said. "I'd hate to think of them coming up into our house during the night. Where do they live?"

"As Milo explained to me, they live in the ruins just out beyond where the new upper city has been built. There the rubble is loose and air gets down, even a little light in the daytime."

"I still don't see how it is possible for you to go down and not be seen by the mutants," father commented.

"My friend Milo lives in that border area just about where the mutants find it possible to live. By approaching him from this direction, I am not likely to meet any mutants. The air is not as good there and they avoid going there. Milo told me it would be safe if I stuck to the path I used originally. It had been made years before and had been abandoned. He said it would be dangerous for me to go beyond where he lives."

Gretta looked at my father and smiled. "I would be very happy if you could give me a boy just like this."

He smiled back.

Suddenly my heart jumped a beat. There was a pounding at the front gate-door. The watch guard!

My father looked at me and motioned toward the basement. I scurried down the steps and into my hidden room, making sure the concealing bricks were carefully replaced.

There I lay with the lights out, all except the blue light which was still burning. Father had not even had time to change the light signals. What was happening upstairs? Why had the watch guard come just then? Was it possible that Gretta, my new mother, had got word to them? It couldn't be. She was too kind and gentle to do such a terrible thing.

I waited and listened. I could hear faint sounds in the basement. Inwardly I groaned in despair. For a few moments upstairs I had thought the worst of my problems were solved. It would be cruel to have them find me now.

I slung my bag of supplies over my shoulder and sat with my feet hanging down in the hole I had dug to the underground. For an hour I sat there. Then the blue light went off and the red light came on. There was still danger above, but at least father had been able to get to the switch he used to control the lights.

At every new imagined sound, my heart began to pound, and I would start to lower myself into the hole. How much good that would do, I had no idea. If the watch guard actually did come into my room and saw where I had gone, they would probably send men down after me.

Unexpectedly the red light went off and the blue came on. Did my father actually want me to come up? This was not like him. If it was safe, he would come to me. I was still too terrified to feel it was safe. I would wait. After a time I heard sounds at the entrance to my room. They were familiar sounds, the kind my father always made.

When his head finally came through, he was all smiles. "It was the watch guard all right. They've come and gone. And Gretta said not a word."

"But why did they come tonight?" I asked.

"In our talking to you, I forgot the time. Our lights were the only ones on in the street. The guard stopped to check. I should have known better, but I was so excited having you meet Gretta."

"The guard—they are really gone?"

"Yes, they merely wanted to know why our lights were on. Gretta came up with a perfectly reasonable explanation. She said she and I had just been mated and we were re-reading the rules and regulations. That seemed to satisfy them although, as usual, they made a search of the whole house."

He looked at me with a questioning expression. "How do you like Gretta?"

"I like her very much." Then I added—"I'll try to be a good son to her."

"The best way to do that is to keep from being discovered. You know, of course, that if you are found out, both Gretta and I will be condemned to death for hiding you."

I nodded that I understood.

After he left, I bathed and slipped into my bed. After the hard metal bed of the night before, this was wonderfully soft. I quickly dropped off into a deep, dreamless sleep.

For the next four days I stayed close to my room. Twice I went up during the daytime and ran around the yard. Although it was still winter and the air brisk and cool, the snow had gone. I would not have dared make footprints if there had been a snow cover on the ground.

I even checked over my miniature cave in the garden and made plans for deepening it so that I could run and hide there when spring came and I worked outdoors again.

Each evening when father and Gretta came home from work, I was given a warm dinner. As he had said, she was a good housekeeper and especially a good cook, work she had specialized in in the dormitory. Many people in Resurrection City didn't bother to grow their own food. They lived entirely on the food pellets which they could have merely by pressing a button connected to a pneumatic tube that came from central headquarters to each house. The pellets were available on a generous quota basis. Because we didn't depend on them entirely, I was able to save out a number. I felt that Milo could use them.

On the fifth day I packed up my bag of supplies with as many pellets as I had been able to save and made ready to return to the area below. The climb down this time was much less frightening. Now I knew where I was going and what to expect. I made sure I marked each crossing of the tunnels.

I was surprised how little time it took to reach the room where I had seen Milo. I suspected this was not where he lived. Except for this spot I had no other clue as to where to go to find him. I would have to wait here and let him find me.

I lay down on the old metal bed and looked up. I was surprised to see literally hundreds of spots of lights overhead. Sunlight was coming in. The rubble here must be very loose and open. The air, too, was better than back under the denseness below Resurrection City.

I waited in silence, my light out, wondering when Milo would begin my lessons. I knew that secretly I had envied Ralf going to training school. Now, I would have the same advantages. Maybe even better. At least I didn't expect that Milo would fill me with the lies about mutants that Resurrection boys and girls probably had to hear.

After about two hours of waiting, I grew restless. What if Milo had forgotten about me? What if something had happened to him?

I got to my feet and picked up my torch. Milo had warned me that to go beyond this point could be dangerous for me. Before switching on the light, I made an effort to find if I could see without it. The light filtering in from far overhead was dim, not much better than starlight. But I did find that I could distinguish large objects. I decided to use this natural light and try to feel my way forward. The torch, I knew, would make me an instant target for mutants if they spotted it.

Fumbling my way along, I grew conscious of a low humming sound ahead. As I came closer, I recognized it as a chorus of young voices repeating something in unison. In the darkness it had an eerie effect.

Even more carefully now I moved forward. Finally I saw a tiny glimmer of light. It was around a corner. I put one eye to the edge.

There, with a dozen or so children sitting in a half circle around him, was Milo. He had a slate blackboard and was pointing to a group of words that he had written there. The children repeated the words. Milo's cat, Witch, lay curled up at his feet.

What struck me with wonder were the children. It was my first sight of mutant boys and girls. About half of them looked normal. Perhaps they had hidden defects like I had. But the rest—I shuddered to see them.

One had a completely hairless head, with oversize eyes and no chin at all. Another raised four hands at the same time to attract Milo's attention. Another had almost no face at all, merely a round ball-like shape. Still another had red, angry-looking knobs all over its elongated head, with two long fangs sticking out of its mouth.

I stepped back so that I could not possibly be seen. I hardly dared move for fear I would make a sound. For an hour I stood there, motionless and rigid with fright. Yet I was fascinated too. Those mutant children out there were getting a lesson in reading. Soon, I, too, would be getting my lesson. How long would it take me to learn to read and write? A week? A month? Perhaps Milo would speed up the lessons for me. What had he meant by training me to take his place? I suppose he intended that I should become the teacher. But no—he had said something about my becoming the new teacher-leader when I was eighteen. I was confused by all these thoughts which really made no sense.

I heard a shuffling sound from the class area. I peeked around again. The last of the mutant children was limping off, dragging a third dangling leg behind him. Horrible!

I started to step out into view, but behind his back I could see Milo waving frantically for me to stay hidden. I kept my eyes on him.

At that instant he half straightened up his crippled back and held out his hands to someone who had just come into the area. It was someone who was still out of range of my vision. The person moved forward toward Milo.

It was a young man, not very tall but strongly built, handsome in a way, although his mouth was thin and his eyes shone with a kind of cruel ferocity. Too curious to move back any farther, I stayed at the corner and peered out.

I was amazed to see him get down on his knees and put his forehead on the ground in front of the cat. Then he got up, and with bowed head stood before Milo.

"What message does Witch have for me today?" he asked.

Milo frowned at the young man. "You are too eager, Trax. Your time will come. But not yet. You must be patient."

"I have been patient for many months now. I ask again—what does Witch say for me to do?"

Milo glanced down at the cat at his feet, its gray-green eyes fixed on the young man, its whole body coiled up as though ready to spring at him.

"As you know, Trax, Witch talks only to me. No one else can understand her. I will talk to her again. Come back next week. I may have some word for you then."

"As always you ask me to wait . . . always next week!

Tell Witch I won't wait much longer. If she won't tell me what I must do and when, I will do it without her word. Tell her that."

"I'll tell her, Trax. I must warn you though—she does not like to be hurried. Come back next week. But don't be too hopeful. Remember Witch knows all. She knows when it will be best for you to do what you have to do. To do other than she advises could mean disaster for you. Remember your brother, Bonner. He thought he knew better than Witch. Look what happened to him —shot by the watch guard."

Milo touched the young man on the shoulder and said, "I know how hard it is for you to wait. I have waited thirty years. I am still waiting."

"I won't wait thirty years," Trax said hoarsely. He turned to go. "I'll be back next week. Witch had better have a message for me then."

As soon as he had gone, Milo turned awkwardly away from the chair he had been leaning on. For the first time I realized how badly crippled he was. He moved with a slow, sliding motion, almost a sideways glide.

"I heard you come up, Rolf," he said. "I was afraid the children would hear you too. They develop good hearing down here in the quiet of the lower city. That's why I had them recite more than usual. Come, Rolf, we'll go now to my real hiding place. Not even the mutants know where it is. Your first lesson is due."

"How about that young man?" I asked. "The one who bowed to Witch and asked for her advice."

"I'll have to tell him something when he comes next week. He is one of the very few hot-headed ones I have to contend with—eager to go up and kill people in the upper city. He is a trouble-maker. But as long as I have Witch, I think I can control him and the few others like him."

"How is that?"

"These people are highly superstitious. To them Witch really has supernatural powers. It is my way to hold the more rebellious mutants in check."

"What happens when Witch dies?"

"A good question. It would probably be my own death too. But now to the lessons. . . ."

XI

In the maze of rubble that made up the city below the city, Milo had a haven of his own that offered the utmost in protection. He explained to me that it had originally been a bank, a place where money and other valuables were kept. He said that because of its unusually strong construction, the various rooms were still more or less intact. He even showed me stacks of paper money from the old regime.

The rooms he used were unlike any I had ever seen. Altogether there were about ten different spaces which he said constituted his private domain. Each room had walls which were amazingly thick and strong. They were covered with a stone-like veneer, but I could see the steel plate below.

Best of all, Milo pointed out, approach to the area was very difficult to find. The entrance had been blocked by a heavy crush of stone and metal beams and tile. Only by going around to the rear and sliding through a series of confusing and very narrow passageways was access possible.

"This is where I live," Milo said as he led me around from room to room. He stopped in front of a huge, round metal door. "This is the only place I have not been able to enter. It's what they called a vault. They kept their main store of money here. It was closed and locked at the time of the destruction. It has stayed locked ever since."

I ran my hand across the smooth metal of the vault door, still shiny and new-looking after seventy years. I spun the wheel at the center.

"That wheel is the secret for opening it," Milo said.

"So many times one way; so many times the other; and so on. In a locked desk I found a number list. My guess is that it is the first half of the combination series. Someone else probably had the second half. I have never been able to get it right. Anyway the money in the vault is no good."

He took me to the room he said he actually lived in. He had been carrying a candle. Suddenly he blew it out. For a long minute there was complete blackness. Then I heard him move and an electric light flashed on overhead.

"It is the only electrical connection in the whole of Destruction City. Through some kind of fluke, the bank's wiring system has contact with the power source in Resurrection City. I have no way of checking back to see where the connection is—not in my crippled condition. But there it is—a light."

He looked up at it proudly. "I use it to read by. And now that you are here, you too can use it to read by."

I glanced around. "How about water and food? I brought you some extra food pellets."

"One question at a time, Rolf. Water is no problem. We have miles of old imperishable plastic water pipes available. Some of the mutants have become quite skilled in hooking up our piping to the Resurrection City water mains.

"Food is a more serious matter. And I do thank you for the food pellets you bring me. Some of our more agile and brave mutants make forays into the food storehouses. As time goes by it becomes increasingly difficult to steal the food we need. Also our numbers have increased."

"Where does the food come from?"

"There are fields surrounding the city. They are worked by robot machines under the control of Class Two guards. The raw products are brought into the city and processed into pellets."

"How do you yourself get your food?"

Milo had seated himself in a metal chair. Witch jumped into his lap. He caressed its soft fur.

"This," he said, "is how I get my food. Witch, as you must have realized my now, is looked on by the mutants as one who can foretell the future. She is worshipped as something supernatural, able to advise them on matters of all kinds."

"Is she really able to look into the future?" I asked, peering again at the animal.

Milo smiled. "You'll never find anyone better able to look into the future."

Somehow the answer didn't quite ring true. But to play it safe I reached out and rubbed Witch behind the ears. She purred contentedly.

"Now for the lessons," Milo said. "First I want to learn what you already know. . . ."

And so for two days and two nights I sank wearily into the morass of learning that Milo tried to have me absorb. I would never learn. The alphabet was easy. Mother had taught me that much. But using them in words and using words in sentences—this was more than my mind could grasp so quickly.

I felt numb and utterly defeated at the end of the first two-day period. When my time came for returning to my secret room, I faced Milo with tears in my eyes.

"I'll never learn," I said in dismay. "I've spent two whole days and I still don't know how to read or write."

Milo's gentle face broke out in a broad smile. "You are by far the best beginning student I have ever had. As for not learning how to read and write in two days, I'll be very happy if you can learn to read simple things in a year and to write much of anything in two or three years."

"Two or three years!" I exclaimed.

Milo chuckled again. "And I'll be more than delighted if you can read and write well by the time you are eighteen."

"And now," he added, "I want you to take these lesson sheets back with you. For the next five days I want you to go over and over them until you know them perfectly."

I pointed to a wall where books covered the entire surface. "When will I be able to take one of these and read it?"

He put his hand on my head. "Learning," he said, "is a long, hard road. And like every road in life, it starts with taking a few first steps. These lessons are your first steps. The books will be yours to read when you are ready for them."

When I picked up my bag and stood ready to go, I asked—"How will I find my way back to the passage-way?"

"Witch will show you the way. Remember, Witch knows everything."

He was laughing heartily as I followed the cat back through the twists and turns until I reached a place I recognized. I turned to pat Witch in thanks but she had disappeared.

Back in my room I found the red light burning.

I felt helpless. What had happened while I was gone? Had something bad occurred that made it unsafe for me to come up? Father knew I was due back at this time. Perhaps he wanted to be sure I didn't come dashing up and stumble into trouble. But how I wanted to tell him and my new mother of all that had happened to me.

For a whole day and a night, I stayed in my room. I fretted and worried. I even had trouble sleeping. I went over the lessons Milo had given me—over and over—hundreds of times until I thought I would go mad.

Finally, on the second day, even though the red light

was still burning, I slipped out into the basement and moved cautiously up the stairs.

I could hear nothing. The house seemed to be empty. I hurried to the front to look out at the gate-door. It was closed. I had already passed through the kitchen and front room. I went to the room where father and Greta slept. The door was closed. I pressed my ear to it and listened. I thought I heard a groan.

Slowly I opened the door. It was dark within. I could barely see that someone was in the bed.

"Is that you, Gretta?" my father's voice sounded weakly.

"No, it's Rolf."

"Oh, no, Rolf. It's not safe for you here. I'm sick."

I moved into the room leaving the door open. Enough light came in for me to see that my father was really very ill. He lay there panting for breath.

"Suddenly I can't breathe," he said in a gasp.

"What can I do?" I cried in desperation.

"Nothing, Rolf. Go back to your room."

I looked around. I had to do something, anything. I'd lost my mother and Ralf. I couldn't risk losing my father too. But what could I do? I felt completely and utterly helpless.

He gazed up at me with pain-stricken eyes. Then he began to choke again. His breathing came in short gasps that I could tell gave him a great deal of pain. He needed help . . . the kind of help I couldn't give him.

I'd have to alert the watch guard. But how?

I ran to the front gate-door. I opened it and looked down the street. For once I was glad to see a watch guard squad coming at its usual slow pace.

I opened the gate-door and left it wide open. Then I hurried back to the house. There, I left the front door open also.

I waited for the watch guard to come even with our house and then let out a deep moan. From the darkness of the interior I could see out without being seen by them.

The officer in charge of the squad stopped his men. I could see him motioning for them to enter. I sprinted to my father's door and opened it. Then I headed for the basement stairs and down to my room.

Almost petrified with fear that I was losing my father, I sat in my room hour after hour staring at the still burning red light.

No, it could not be. My father was so strong, so good. My torment built up until I felt I couldn't stand it any longer. I wanted to butt my head against the wall. Or scream in terror. Or push aside the barriers that held me in this lonely room.

Suddenly I became aware of something new. In my delirium, I couldn't at first identify what was different. And yet bit by bit I became aware that something had changed. Then it came to me—the blue light was burning!

I dashed for the opening into the basement. I rushed up the stairs. What did it matter any more if it were a trap! I had to know about my father! I had to know!

XII

I was breathless when I stumbled up into the kitchen. Gretta, my new mother, was at the stove.

"I put on the blue light," she said with a smile. "I thought you ought to have something hot and nourishing to eat."

"Father—how is he?" I blurted out.

"He's going to be fine. By some kind of miracle, the watch guard found the gate-door open and came in. Your father was choking. They rushed him to the medical center. I don't know what they did there to stop the choking. But they did. He is going to be all right."

I plopped down in a chair and started to sob in relief. Gretta came over and put her arms around me. For a moment I thought it was my own mother comforting me. It felt good. The warmth of her body next to mine gave me strength to look up into her face. Father had said she was homely. All I could see there was beauty, the beauty of love and tenderness.

"Best that you eat something now," she said as she hustled back to the stove to make up a plate of hot food for me.

I knew there were tear stains on my cheeks as I ate. I didn't care. Father was going to be all right. And Gretta was showing me that she loved me and was willing to share my danger.

I told her about Milo and his cat and the strange place where he lived.

After I had eaten, I said to Gretta that it would be safest for both of us if I went back to my basement room. She agreed. She said she would signal me with the lights when it was safe for me to come up. I especially urged her to put on the blue light when my father came home and it was safe for me to see him.

Back in my room, I quickly took a shower and slipped into bed. Within minutes I was asleep.

In the morning I awoke with the feeling that I would know today about my father. The red light was burning but that was as I expected. Gretta, I knew, had to work and while she was gone and there was a possibility of my father being brought back, it would be best for me to stay quietly out of sight.

I kept watching the clock on my viviscreen. Some two or three hours before Gretta was due to come home, the blue light went on. This was so unexpected that I pondered for several minutes whether or not to go on up. It might be that Gretta had come home early and had news of father. Or it might be that father himself had returned. At any rate, I knew I had to find out.

Cautious as ever, I made my way up the stairs. All was quiet. I went immediately to my father's room. He was lying on the bed, smiling as I came in.

"Rolf," he said, "you saved my life. I would have choked to death in a short time more. I can only guess what you did to attract the attention of the watch guard. But it worked. They did ask me how it was the front gate-door had been left open contrary to rules. I knew you must have done it. I said I did, hoping they would see it and come in. They believed me. I'm all right now. I'll even be able to go back to work in a day or two."

I sank down on the edge of the bed and took up his hand. "Gretta was wonderful," I said. "I'm glad she is your new mate."

He smiled. "Yes, I'm glad too." His smile broadened. "You may as well know. She is going to have a baby. How would you like a brother or sister?"

"Will it be like Ralf or like me?"

Father's face clouded over. "I wish I knew."

To cheer him up, I told him about the lessons I had

started with Milo. I assured him I was in little danger from the mutants as long as I followed the paths Milo had established for me. I even described the place where he lived—the steel-walled rooms, the huge vault with its round door, the stacks of books which the mutants had dug up in the ruins and had brought to him.

Then I told him how a young man, a mutant, had come threatening action against the people of the upper city, but that Milo's cat was his weapon against such violence.

Finally I related what Milo said he had in store for me —another dozen years of schooling to get me ready to be the new teacher-leader of the mutants.

This bit of news was hard for my father to accept. He started to tell me how horrible it would be for a son of his to side with the mutants, possibly even lead them in rebellion against the upper city. As he talked, however, he began to falter. He looked at me strangely.

"After all," he said, "you are a mutant too. Your whole life has been ruined because of the hatred for mutants that we have been brought up on. If anyone has the right to side in with them, you have. I can only hope that if you do become their leader, you can hold them back from violence."

"I think that is what Milo wants me to do."

"Rolf," my father said as he pressed my hand warmly, "I hope that some day both normal people and mutants can live together in peace and harmony, as friends. No upper city. No lower city. Just one city for both. I don't know how it could be worked out. But it is what I hope for."

We both heard the sound at the same instant. I rushed to the front door and looked out. It was Gretta coming home from work. She was alone so I waited for her to come in.

She kissed me and then hurried into the bedroom

when I told her that father was home. The way they embraced I could see there was real love there.

Quietly I slipped out for a walk around the yard. The walls were as high and formidable as ever. I could sense, however, that the worst of the winter was over. There was that feeling in the soil under my feet that foretold an early spring. Somehow I would find time to help in the garden. It was the least I could do for my new mother.

Later, after Gretta had prepared a hot dinner for the three of us, I went back to my room. This time I gave real attention to the lessons Milo had given me to study. My mind, now at ease, began to see the pattern of the studies.

Two days later I went back down below for another learning session. The first thing Milo said to me when I reached his place of refuge was about his cat. "Rolf, when you were last here, you asked what would happen to my control over the mutants when Witch died. It got me to thinking. My control didn't start until I found Witch as a kitten about a dozen years ago. Cats don't live much longer than that, possibly two or three years. There is a good possibility my hold over the mutants will end when Witch dies. I mustn't let that happen."

He looked at me pensively. "Do you think you could have your father get a male cat so we could mate it with Witch?"

"I could ask him. We have never had a cat. In fact, Witch is the first cat I have ever seen. When I go back up, I'll find out if he can get one."

Milo smiled. "Witch is something supernatural to the mutants. If we could mate her with a tomcat without them even knowing about it, when Witch has her babies, they'll think they too are gifted with supernatural powers. I'll select a female from the litter and tell the mutants that Witch is training her to be the new Witch when she dies."

I looked at Milo in surprise. "Then Witch really doesn't have supernatural powers?"

"Of course she does, Rolf. All cats have. And especially Witch."

That evening, after I had shown Milo what I had learned from my lessons, I told him what my father had said about normal people and mutants living together in peace.

He sat for some time, merely running his hand gently across Witch's sleek fur. Then he spoke—

"I too hope that some day we will all live together in peace and harmony. That, indeed, is why I am pinning great hopes on you, Rolf, to be the leader who shows the way."

"But is it possible?

"It doesn't seem so now. There is a growing number of young men like Trax, and mutant girls too, who are eager to do all the damage they can. At the moment I tell them that Witch says it will only lead to their own death. I have tried to get them involved in clearing out new areas, finding access to new food supplies, training some to care for people who become ill, anything to divert them from violence. But some day, they are certain to disobey me. In some ways I can only sympathize with them. They are a lost people, hopeless, crushed, hungry, miserable."

He paused . . . .

"And from what I have heard, it's not much better up above. Your people up there have an obsession for walls. Your homes are surrounded by them. At first the walls were merely a way to use up the vast piles of brick and other building materials that came from the destruction of the old city. But they became a part of the psychology of the survivors. The walls shut people out as well as shut them in. Each home became an isolated unit. Neighborliness disappeared. People became afraid of the families on each side of them. Walls became a

75

frame of mind, a way of life. It would have been better if the survivors had not tried to build their new city on top of the old.

"Resurrection City is nothing but a grid of walls—walls separating people, keeping them from loving and trusting one another. One excuse for the walls was that they offered protection for each family from the possibility of attack by the mutants. This has always been the great fear."

"But the walls around the homes wouldn't stop the mutants if they really invaded the upper city," I said.

"True. But when people get a passion for walls around them, it is a sign of fear. Walls are the only defense they can think of to shield them from the nightmare horrors of a mutant invasion.

"Even the walls around the city itself, I feel, are not so much to protect against whatever foes could come from the forests outside as to keep the people safely inside. Or what they think of as safety.

"Only when the walls come down all over Resurrection City is there any hope for our dream of mutants and normal people living together in peace. And I don't altogether mean the walls of brick."

"What other kinds of walls are there?" I asked.

"The same kinds of walls we have down here in Destruction City. Mental walls. Walls within walls. Walls of prejudice and hatred and fear. Those are the real walls we must try to pull down, Rolf. Yes, my boy, those are the walls you and I must try to pull down."

At this point Witch left Milo's lap and came next to me, rubbing against my leg.

Milo laughed. "Witch says she is in on this too. In fact she gives us a warning."

"A warning?"

"Yes, she says what we plan is full of danger. Death and pain and sorrow lie ahead. The path we take is full of troubles."

"Does she say we will win in the end?"

Milo shook his head. "She says she cannot see further than her own life. We will not win during her lifetime. She does say, however, that the next Witch may see us win through."

"That is all the more reason," I said then, "for me to get a mate for her soon."

PART TWO

WALLS OF LOWER CITY

XIII

I held out my arm as a signal to the three youths with me to stay back out of sight. I crouched down and waited. I knew that my gray tunic made me almost invisible in the half dark only dimly lit by a setting moon. I knew also that my best weapon was surprise.

For several nights I had come to this spot. I had found that the food storehouse here was guarded by only one member of the watch guard. In a few minutes this guard would be making his rounds past where I lay hidden. When he came, I would strike . . . .

I felt a tingling in my body as the tension grew. This was my first real chance to prove my right to leadership of the mutants. Not that there was any real doubt about it.

Just a month ago, Milo had called a meeting of the mutant leaders. At this their first sight of me, he introduced me—almost as if by magic—as his successor and the new Master of Witch. It was what he had promised he would do nearly a dozen years before when I first came to him as a boy of six.

So much had happened. Living mostly in the secret room in my father's house, working in the garden, eating Gretta's cooked food, I had grown tall and strong. I thought with pity of the three young mutant males who had come with me on this food foray—weak, undersized, dull and listless. Yes, I had every right to be their leader. This raid to the upper level to get food would show the people of Destruction City that I was their superior in every way.

Waiting in the dark for the guard to come, I thought back over those twelve years. Gretta's baby had been born, a beautiful girl, normal in every respect. When she was about three, she had a sister. Both little girls had been taken from a grief-stricken Gretta when each reached six. And the years rolled on . . . .

More and more I had come to stay longer periods with Milo. Witch had died. One of her kittens had grown up to look just like her. I don't believe the mutants ever knew of the change when the new young Witch was shown to them.

My lessons, too, had gone steadily forward until Milo's health began to fail. Then he merely turned me loose in his library and gave me a schedule to read the books by categories. That way I plunged with delight into the various fields of knowledge, reading everything Milo had on a subject before going on to the next. What brilliant, learned people our ancestors of the Twentieth Century must have been. Too brilliant, of course, for their own good.

I was glad that Milo, fading in health as he was and showing his age, had been able to make a big show when, with a flourish, he brought me before the mutants as the new Master of Witch. I was wearing a coat of mail which Milo had made for me. It was completely covered with gold coins of the old regime.

With only the first half of the numbers, he had experimented for years with the dial on the huge vault door. One day he had hit upon the last half of the combination. Except for huge amounts of now worthless paper money and documents and a few bags of silver coins, the gold coins were the only items of value he found. They did make a colorful and impressive jacket.

Yes, the years had been good to me. I wondered whether my twin brother, Ralf, had fared as well. He would be eighteen now, too. Probably in the Class Two rating by now.

And Elissa? She was a month or two younger than Ralf and I. She would not be quite eighteen yet. Somehow, in all the years since I had watched her play in the yard next to our house, I had never entirely forgotten her. The long blond hair. The eager, happy expression. The slender body which even at six showed all the promise of the beauty she would one day be.

With effort I pulled my mind away from remembrance of the one sight I had ever had of her naked body. I must not forget why I was here now—a mutant myself, heading my first raid on a Resurrection City food storehouse.

The time for the guard to come was drawing closer . . . .

Then I heard his measured footsteps. I knew that a frontal challenge would be fatal. Each guard carried a laser gun. One touch from its beam would bring instant death. Through the years scores of mutants had died on raids like this. I had no intention of giving up my life in this way.

I crouched lower . . . .

When the guard came opposite my hiding place, I tossed a pebble out past him. I knew he would turn in that direction instinctively to see what it was. In one leap I was on his back. I could hear the laser gun clatter down on the ground. My arm tightened around his throat and I squeezed. When I felt his body go limp, I let him fall.

The three youths had run up. One of them carried a cord with which I bound the unconscious guard. The mutants would have killed him but I had made it clear to them before we started there would be no killing. To prevent him from calling for help when he regained his senses, I fixed a gag in his mouth.

Two of my partners had brought steel prying bars. We knew that the doors of the storehouse were metal and heavily locked. They could be pried open, however, if enough pressure was applied.

For an hour we struggled to force open the door. By the time we had succeeded, we still had two hours of leeway before the guard replacement was scheduled to arrive. We needed every bit of that time to carry the boxes of prepared food pellets back to the spot where we planned to cache them. Almost up to the time when the new guard was to come, the four of us lugged the boxes to the collection place where others were to pick them up later.

Before leaving, I went back to the guard I had attacked. He was conscious and struggling violently to break free of his bonds. Looking down at him, I realized that his uniform might come in handy in some future raid, along with the laser gun which I had picked up earlier.

I knew I had only a few minutes left. I sent my three raid-partners back to the safety of the lower city. Again I squeezed the guard's throat until he gasped and I felt him collapse. Quickly I loosened the bonds and stripped him.

Just as I was gathering up the uniform into a bundle, I heard the replacement guard. He was hurrying as though late, or possibly alarmed at not being met. I moved back into the shadows.

The replacement guard went rushing by me, almost stumbling over the nude body of the guard on the ground. He halted, his electric torch, beam directed downward. I heard him cry out in alarm. Then the beam went around in a wide circle.

I dodged down and the light passed over my head. I had the laser gun in my hand, but I wanted no killing. After a moment or two, the guard turned off his light and ran off, his feet pounding heavily on the pathway.

I smiled. After only a month since being introduced to the mutants. I had pulled off my first food raid. I knew how desperate was the need for more food. Now they would have some. . . .

XIV

If there had been any hesitation among the mutants to accept me, the raid had settled their doubts. The food pellets we had stolen would supply the needs of Destruction City for almost a month.

After so many years of lonely isolation and hiding, it was good to be among people who looked up to me as their leader . . . even if they were mutants.

The first thing I did when I got back to the lower city after the raid was to go to Milo. For months he had been declining. I had fed him and bathed him. I could see that the end was not far ahead.

"How was the raid?" he asked when I had made my way through the secret passageways into his private area.

"We took all we could carry in two hours. It was a good raid."

"No one hurt?"

I shook my head. "I used the trick you had shown me, squeezing the muscles on the guard's throat. I don't think I hurt him."

"That's good, Rolf." Milo said in a hoarse whisper. "Although the guards are in Class Two, they are really slaves of the true rulers in Class One. Those are your real enemies. Eliminate them and the problem could be solved in a generation."

"You think it would take a generation?"

"Yes, Rolf. Remember, long ago, we talked about the walls of prejudice and hate and fear that have been erected both in Resurrection City and down here in Destruction City? It will take a generation, maybe longer, to pull down those walls. And I feel strongly that the Class One rulers are the biggest obstacle."

"Who are they? What are they like?"

"I wish I could tell you, Rolf. It would help you to have some knowledge of who and what they are. All I know is that a number of the leading scientists who survived the war formed a group to rule the city. They developed a type of brain operation which gave them absolute control over those who had it, the Class Two people. These rulers have kept themselves secluded. Their descendants now run everything from their head-quarters building in the center of Resurrection City. No one ever sees them. But they are the ones who pro-more the hatred and fear of mutants that dominates life in the upper city."

He coughed heavily for a few minutes, then said in a rasping voice, "Bring me Witch."

I called. She came quickly to me. I handed her to Milo. He started to mumble. The words made little sense except that it seemed to me he was talking to the new Witch as though he thought it was the original Witch. His mind, I had long known, was fading.

Finally he released the cat and it lay quietly on the cover next to him.

"The time has come," he said weakly, "for you to leave me and go live among the mutants. To be their leader, they must know you. I was not a mutant and never could live among them. I used Witch to protect me. But you are a mutant. Now, with Witch, you have double protection."

"I can't leave you. You would die."

"I'm going to die anyway. Don't you see, Rolf, I have finished what I began. You are ready to lead. My task is done. Now leave me."

I started up to get him a drink of water. For some time I had known that this would happen. I knew it was inevitable. That didn't make it any easier to accept.

How could I go on without Milo, my teacher, my friend, my conscience?

When I came back with the cup of water, I saw that the last flicker of life had gone out of him. His hand still rested on Witch's warm body.

Impulsively I picked her up and ran as fast as I could through the new familiar passageways to the heart of Destruction City. As I ran I could hear people stop their work and follow behind me.

When I reached the place where they held their meetings, I leaped up in a small platform and held Witch high overhead. I stood there for several minutes, holding her there, until I felt enough people had come.

I lowered Witch into the hollow of my left arm. With my right arm I motioned for all to fall to their knees. "Witch," I shouted, "tells me that Milo is dead! You will never see him again!"

From their knees, the people looked up at me in surprise, waiting for my next words.

"But fear not!" I cried out. "As the new Master of Witch, I am able to understand what she says. Milo is dead. But I live . . . and through me you will hear what Witch counsels you to do!"

I stepped down, and with heavy heart made my way back through the maze of tunnels in the rubble. I found Milo as I had left him. I searched through the pocket of his tunic and found the combination figures he had discovered to open the vault door. Somewhere I had read that our ancestors had buried their heroes and leaders in burial vaults. Milo deserved no less a burial.

I went to the huge round vault door and began to spin the wheel, following the instructions he had written down. Heavy as the door was, it swung open with almost no effort on my part. I went inside and looked around. What a fortune the piles of paper money must have represented at one time. I did no more than glance at them.

Where to place Milo's withered old body? The interior of the vault was highly polished stainless steel. Finally I spread several stacks of paper money out on the floor. It was on this once-great accumulation of wealth that I placed him.

Then I went out and closed the door, spinning the wheel until I knew that it was securely locked again. I took the slip containing the combination and tore it into many tiny pieces.

I looked around. I would come back here often. Although I had read all the books Milo had collected, I wanted to be able to reread many of them over and over again. Now I realized my place was with the mutants.

I picked up Witch and together we went back to the communal center. I felt that the people were looking at me now in a new light. I offered them all that Milo had given them . . . and something more. Youth. And strength. And a hope for better things.

First I went to Trax, now middle-aged, his rebellious spirit largely held back by his added years and the fact that he had assumed a degree of leadership responsibilities among the mutants.

"Trax," I said, "I need a place to live . . . a place somewhere near the center of Destruction City."

He smiled. "I'll find a place for you, a warm cozy place." Because of his early boldness and energy, he had become the acknowledged head of the mutants, bowing only to Milo. Although not as big or as strong as I was, he was a dominant male among the relatively weak denizens of the lower city. I knew, from observing him glaring at me, that he didn't like me. But he was intensely superstitious and I felt he feared me.

The people of Destruction City lived in burrows dug into the mass of rubble from the old city. Many of these cave-like places were only a short distance below the top level. This gave them light and air. Where Trax took me, however, was not up to one of these more desirable locations. Instead he showed me a room-space that was large enough and well equipped with a rebuilt bed and two chairs. But it was at a much lower level.

"This is near the communal center," he said. He hesitated before leaving. "Is there anything I can bring you? Anything at all?"

As he said this, he smiled broadly. I felt he was hiding something from me. What, I didn't know. Perhaps I was only imagining it.

First I fed Witch and gave her a drink. Then, indifferently, I chewed on a food pellet. Somehow, I thought, I would have to find ways to get fresh foods for these people. Too long they had merely survived on stolen prepared pellets.

I bathed in the tiny shower stall. Then, as was my custom, I slipped naked into my bed.

For some time I lay thinking. Milo was gone. I was now to carry on his work. I was to be the voice of Witch. The mutants desperately needed forceful leadership. But what was I to do? Not even Milo had been able to do more than keep them alive. Somehow I would have to develop plans for bettering their conditions. And somehow, too, I would have to develop the wisdom and the courage to carry them out.

I was now committed, utterly and completely, to life among these miserable people. Their ways would have to become my ways. Their fate, my fate. No longer could I go back to my father's house for long periods of time although I knew that I would periodically check on my father and Gretta. I loved them and they loved me. They had protected me and saved my life. If real conflict ever came between the upper and lower cities, I would make every effort to see that they were kept safe from harm.

Musing thus and almost half asleep, I suddenly became wide awake. . . .

There was someone in my room! I could sense it. At

first I thought it must have been a slight sound that had alerted me. Then I realized it was an odor, a fragrance.

In the intense darkness of the lower-city room space to which Trax had brought me, all I could do was listen and use my sense of smell.

Carefully I slid my legs over the edge of my narrow bed and started to rise to my feet. A hand touched my bare shoulder. Another hand touched my cheek. They were soft, warm hands, the hands of a girl.

A girl! Was this what Trax meant when he asked me if there was anything he could bring me?

I seized the slender wrists and held them firmly in my hands.

"No! No!," a low, gentle voice said. "You are hurting me."

The fragrance grew stronger.

"Who are you? What do you want?" I asked, keeping my voice low but insistent.

"Don't you want me? It is not right for our new Master of Witch to sleep alone. I bring you only joy."

"You haven't answered me," I said, still holding tight to the wrists. "Who sent you?"

"What does it matter? I am here. Do not send me away. Please release my hands. Put your arms around me. Let me put my arms around you."

A soft body pressed itself up against me, in spite of the wrist-holding. The fragrance grew stronger still. Then—like a bolt of lightning—a thought struck me! What if she were a monster, a hideous monstrosity? I would have to know.

With a violent heave, I pushed her away. Quickly I reached around for my bag of supplies. I felt for my electric torch. But by the time I had found it and had sent its beam around the space, she had gone.

I groaned. Now I would never know. My blood was pounding as I went back to my bed. Now, at least, I knew one thing—I had normal physical desires. The touch of the girl's hand on my bare shoulder, the feel of her body against mine, her fragrance—all had stirred me as I had never been stirred before. Too long I had suppressed all such feelings.

Who was the girl? Would she be one of those with only a minor defect like my own four-toed feet? Or would she be one of those so hideous one could hardly look at them?

And Trax?

Could this have been something he had arranged? His parting words had implied that he was ready to provide more than just a sleeping place for me. Did he mean a sleeping partner as well? What could he hope to gain by it? Or had some girl on her own decided to come to me in the night?

At any rate this was a new problem I had to solve. I grinned sheepishly as I slipped under the covers. It might even be a pleasurable problem, I thought to myself, as I wondered what would have happened if I hadn't had that idiotic idea about monsters.

XV

I woke up the next morning to a full realization that I now had almost overwhelming responsibilities. At eighteen I was thrust into a position of leadership for which I did not feel myself really qualified. Possibly Milo had meant to spend this past year teaching me the principles of how to lead people. But he had been too ill, his mind too vague and wandering.

Now he was gone. And I was, at least for the moment, the head of Destruction City.

I knew, of course, as Milo had known, that the real source of power over the mutants lay in their superstitious belief in Witch. Milo had played the game for years. Now I would have to learn how to play it.

As I lay on my cot, I tried to review what my most pressing problems were:

* Food for the mutant population, and not only stolen food pellets but fresh food as well.

* Control over the vengeful young people to keep them from making a desperate invasion of the upper city with almost certainty that it would fail.

* General improvement of the deplorable living conditions throughout the lower city.

* Organization of the mutants so that individual skills could be developed, especially in the care of the sick and old.

* An educational system for the mutant children.

These, I knew, were some of the more imminent general problems.

There were personal problems too:

* Trax! I sensed in him a rival for leadership. Under

Milo's declining rule, Trax had grown strong. He would not like to see me take his powers away from him.

* My father and Gretta! Both of their little girls had been taken away from them. The two older folks were alone in the house. Whatever else happened I had to protect them.

* Ralf and Elissa! Perhaps they were gone forever out of my life. Perhaps not. I knew that I thought often of them, wondering about them.

* And not the least of my personal problems, I realized, was what had happened to me the night before. What was I to do about my basic hunger for a mate? Strangely enough, with all the great problems facing me on my first full day among the mutants, this was the one I thought about the most.

I leaped out of bed, showered quickly, and ate a food pellet washed down by a cup of water. I fed and watered Witch.

Then I put the gold coin jacket on over my gray tunic. This was the time for pomp and ceremony. Before leaving my living space, I had a chance, in the candle light, to see a reflection of myself in a strip of mirror a previous occupant had put there. I felt I had to make an impressive appearance.

What I saw was a young man fully half a head taller than the tallest mutant I had ever seen, and a full head taller than average. I had broad shoulders and well muscled arms and legs. In comparison to the half-starved mutants I was almost a giant. I had fair hair which I never let grow too long. My skin was too fair. I had always believed I would be many shades darker if I could live more of my life outdoors under the sun. Much of my face, of course, was covered with a not-very thick growth of beard which I always hoped would grow heavier. Looking at my reflection, I tried to convince myself that young as I was I looked like a leader. But I knew I didn't . . . certainly not in the way Milo did.

Perhaps in time, age would do it for me. The trouble was, my problem was now!

I picked up Witch and strode out to seek Trax. He was not far away. I even suspected he was waiting for me.

"Call a meeting of all the people," I said to him.

He shook his head, apparently getting a secret pleasure out of answering me negatively. "We have no place large enough to hold them all. There are many thousands of us here. Not only that," he added with a sly grin, "at least a fifth of them are unable to move away from their living quarters."

"Call those you consider the most influential," I said then.

He gave me a kind of mocking half bow without letting the smile leave his face.

I strode to the central area where I had told the people of Milo's death the day before. As the minutes went by, the mutants came straggling in . . . the most miserable, misshapen, cowed creatures I had ever seen.

Looking them over, my heart sank. Dull, listless eyes looked up at me. Several had to be carried in in baskets. One legless man pushed himself up front using a small platform on rollers. Red sores covered the faces of many. There were those I had difficulty looking at, so repulsive they were.

Trax had done this deliberately, I realized. If nothing else it showed me his animosity. It also showed me his stupidness. For what it did was make me want all the more to help these poor people. They were now my people! As I stood before them there rose up in me a rising surge of determination to help lead them out of their misery! Nor would I let Trax stop me. . . .

Slowly, with what I hoped was a majestic gesture, I lifted Witch high over my head. The mutants sank to their knees, those that had knees to kneel on. I noticed that Trax was the last to do so. I noticed, too, that close behind him he had a group of about twenty young males, the strongest and ablest of the mutants. I motioned for all to rise.

"Witch gives you her blessing," I said. "Last night she talked to me. There is much she would like to get for you—better food, better living conditions, schooling for your young children, possibly even training some of you in the care of the ill. But she needs your help and your obedience to do her wishes."

I paused to glance at those closest to me. I thought I could discern a flicker of interest and of hope in some of their faces. When I looked over at Trax, however, I could see an obvious smirk of disdain.

Then, for some minutes, I outlined some of the plans Milo and I had often discussed. Because of his infirmity, Milo had not been able to put these plans into effect. Time enough, he would say, when you are their leader.

At the end of my short talk, I said I would be going around throughout the lower city to check on conditions and to make myself available for answering questions.

On the way down from the platform, I motioned for Trax to follow me. For a moment he looked startled, almost frightened. Then he forced a smile and came along behind me.

In my room I took off the gold coin jacket and faced Trax. He was standing, as usual, his eyes fixed on my face. I could see he wanted to be bold but lacked the ultimate courage.

"Did you send that girl here last night?"

The question obviously caught him off guard. Undoubtedly he had expected me to complain about the miserable collection of wretches he had gathered for my 'meeting.' He shook his head vigorously while he fumbled for the right words of denial.

"What girl?" he finally blurted out. "I don't know about any girl." Then once more in control of himself, he smiled. "You want a girl? There are many girls down here who would be glad to share your bed."

I was new to this leadership business. But even I could tell when someone was lying as Trax was lying to me now. I strode over to him and put a firm hand on his upper arm. "When I want a girl, I'll get one for myself, not someone who sneaks in here in the night. Just remember that!"

"But I had nothing to do with any girl coming to you last night."

My grip tightened on his arm. "You lie, Trax. I will not tolerate liars. And don't think you can get away with it by denials. Witch tells me when one lies to me. Why did you do it?"

I could see that he was in a turmoil of doubt. Then a kind of bravado spirit came to his expression. He smiled. "I thought you needed a girl. The leader of Destruction City should have a girl."

"And by supplying me with a girl, you believed you could get into my good graces?" I released my grip on his arm. I knew it was a painful grip for I had squeezed where it would hurt.

"Trax," I said, "I could use your help in managing the affairs of Destruction City. Be a loyal and dependable follower and I will see you keep your present top position. Oppose me, and I will break you."

Like all the mutants who had lived with fear all their lives, Trax, I saw, was truly frightened by my words. I dismissed him. After he had gone, I wondered whether or not I had done the right thing. How much I needed Milo to tell me what to do.

Looking over at Witch as she lay licking her paws, I knew the falseness of claiming that she could talk to me. She gave me no messages, just as she and the original Witch had never really talked to Milo.

I wondered whether superstitious awe of Witch was enough to let me retain control over the mutants. I even had a suspicion that Trax and a few others might be asking themselves if Witch really had supernatural powers such as looking into the future. Just a few bad forecasts and I might find myself in trouble.

Milo had relied on the cat worship. Could I? Perhaps I should prepare for the day when by demonstrating my leadership abilities I could rule without Witch.

I left my room-space and began my inspection trip of Destruction City. It was vaster than I had ever imagined. So much of the area was too tightly compressed with rubble for the mutants to find an easy way to burrow in. As a result, the usable areas were few and sometimes far apart. I found the lower city occupied much of the space not directly under Resurrection City but within the inner walls that marked the extent of the old city that had been destroyed.

Where the mutants lived was in cave-like burrows hardly better than as animals. That's what they were—barely more than animals. No! From the books in Milo's library, pictures showed that animals of the past were usually creatures of grace and beauty. The beings I saw here had little of grace and beauty. Many of them were hideous monstrosities . . . creatures almost too horrible to look at.

And yet they were now my people. These were the mutants of Destruction City to whom I was dedicated to help.

With heavy heart I headed back toward my room-space near the community center. As I drew near I heard a buzz of sound. Turning the last corner I saw ahead a crowd of girls and young women. I could see they had put on their best tunics. Some even had colorful ribbons in their hair. Only about half of them had visible defects such as stunted ears or short arms or legs. The rest, I suspected, had hidden faults as I had.

At my appearance they stopped their chatter. I pointed to one of the girls near me, a dark-haired quite

attractive girl without any obvious defects. I asked—
"What is the meaning of this?"

Flustered at being singled out, she hesitated before answering. Then the words rushed out. "Trax said you wanted to pick your own mate. We have come to let you choose one of us." Her eyes went down, and she added in a faint whisper, "My name is Marda. My fingers are webbed together. That is my only defect."

The other girls rushed past her, eager to tell me what small defects they had. Some seemed ready to strip off their tunics to prove that their bodies were faultless. I couldn't help wondering, as I looked them over, if one of them had been the girl of the night before.

I held up my hands to stop the insistent chattering. Out of the corner of my eye I had seen Witch slinking toward me. I reached over and picked her up. Rubbing behind her ears, I looked around at the group. "As Master of Witch," I proclaimed, trying to keep a straight face, "I shall consult with her. She will tell me if and when and whom to choose. Until then. . . . "

I waved my hand and the girls scurried off.

I sighed. That Marda was a pretty one. . . .

XVI

After spending a week exploring Destruction City and talking with as many of its people as I could, I realized one day that if I were to be able to help them, I would need to know about the upper city.

Trax had more or less avoided me. By contrast I had a hard time avoiding the girls who kept close to my room-space. Merda was usually among them, but less pushy than the others.

It was time I felt for me to get a better idea of what it was really like in Resurrection City. Furthermore, I wanted very much to pay a visit to my father and Gretta.

I dressed myself in the uniform of the guard I had stripped on my first food raid. I knew the guards were able to move about freely, especially at night when Class Three workers were off the streets. My plan was to go up to my old secret room. After I had visited with my father and Gretta and, hopefully, had a warm cooked dinner, I would go out into the upper city to learn whatever I could.

Before leaving my new room-space, I had to take care of another problem—Witch! She had never been left alone. She probably could fend for herself for a day or two. But with me out of the way, it would be almost an open invitation to Trax to steal the cat and proclaim himself as the new Master of Witch. I didn't think he had the courage to do it. On the other hand, there was no point in giving him the opportunity.

I went to the opening leading to the passageway outside. A half dozen girls were talking in whispers just around the corner. I walked around and faced them. I smiled in relief when I saw that Marda was one of them.

The girls stood dumbfounded at my appearing so suddenly before them dressed as a Resurrection City guard. I pretended to look them all over, my gaze even passing over the dark-haired Marda. Then, as though it were just a casual choice, I pointed to her. "Will you come with me?"

Her face grew red as she glanced hurriedly around at the other girls. Her chin was up but her lips were trembling as I preceded her into my room-space.

"Now? You want me now?" she asked weakly as her web-joined fingers fumbled at the belt that held in her tunic.

As I gazed at her standing there before me, starting to remove her garmet, my whole being cried out for her. I wanted her. I wanted to see her naked body. I wanted her to come into my arms. I wanted to have her join her body to mine.

Instead I called Witch to me. When she came up, rubbing against my leg, I picked her up.

"Marda," I said, "I need your help. It is important that I go up to the upper city. There are things I must find out. Someone must take care of Witch while I am gone. Will you do this for me?"

I saw disappointment and relief mingled in her expression as she refastened her belt.

"Witch is easy to handle. Just see that she has food once a day and water to drink. At night she can sleep at the foot of your bed."

I passed the small animal over to the girl. She took Witch gingerly and then, with a rush of affection, pressed the cat to her breast.

"When will you be back?" she inquired, leaving the question implying more than it asked.

"A day. Possibly two."

I waved my hand around the room-space. "You

102

can stay here while I am gone. That's if you want to."

"Yes, I want to," she said eagerly.

I turned to go, but halted at the opening and faced her. "Do not let Witch out of your sight for even one minute. Do not let anyone take her away from you. It is very important."

"Yes, I know," she said in a voice I could hardly hear. "Especially Trax."

I looked at her sharply. When I got back, I would have to question her as to what she might know of Trax's plottings against me, if any.

"Yes," I agreed, "especially Trax. If he tries anything, tell him I will kill him when I return."

She was nodding that she understood what was expected of her when I left her holding Witch in her arms.

The other girls had disappeared. To them, I suppose, they thought I had made my choice. Marda was to be my mate.

But had I really made my choice? True, I felt a great surging hunger to hold Marda in my arms. She was the prettiest of the girls, the one that attracted me the most. Perhaps she had even been the girl who had come to me in the dark that first night. I had never found out who it was. Something told me, however, that she was not that girl. What disturbed me most now was—what did she know about Trax.

I made my way back, through the long passageways, to the room in my father's basement. The red light was burning, not that that really meant very much. It had been father's habit to let it stay on while he was away at work.

I waited until I knew it was time for the two to be coming home. Feeling fairly safe in my guard uniform, I climbed through to the basement and up the stairs. Neither my father nor Gretta had come home as yet.

I stood just inside the front door to keep watch for them. Almost a half hour went by before I saw the gate-door open slowly. I was shocked at sight of my father. While I had been seeing him more or less regularly, I hadn't noticed how much he had aged. He came through the gate, half leaning on Gretta's arm. She, by contrast, seemed to be the stronger of the two.

Not until they had come into the house did I step out to their view. They halted in surprise, obviously startled to see a man in a watch guard uniform in their home.

It was Gretta who recognized me and ran over to throw her arms around me. My father was slower in realizing it was his son, and even then he asked—"Is that you, Ralf?"

I kissed him on the cheek. "No, father. It's not Ralf. It's Rolf. I'm wearing this uniform for protection." I turned to Gretta. "Is it possible to get one of your good cooked meals?"

She nodded happily.

Later, after dinner, the three of us sat in the front room. I told them a bit of what happened to me in the city of the mutants, of Milo's death, the cat worship, and my taking over leadership.

Father viewed me with tired eyes. "Does this mean, Rolf, that the mutants are planning to rise up and attack Resurrection City?"

"Not if I can prevent it."

"Why then do you come in a guard uniform? Is it to spy on us?"

"I came to find out more about the upper city. The mutants need food desperately. Not only food pellets which we steal when we can. Fresh food, too. I feel that if I can help the mutants solve this need, there will be less risk of their rising up. But they are getting more desperate every day. It's a problem that must be solved before we can hope for peace. Tell me, father, all you know how Resurrection City handles its food problem."

"I really know very little," he answered after a time. "There is a high wall surrounding what used to be the limits of the old city. Beyond at some distance is another wall. Between the two walls are fields where all the city's foodstuffs are grown. I have heard that machines do the work. I do know there is a plant in the central area where the raw materials are prepared and processed into pellets. These pellets, as you know, are distributed by pneumatic tube to each house. Reserve supplies of pellets are kept in storehouses at the edge of Resurrection City."

"Yes, father, and it's been a life saver for the mutants. They have tapped a number of the tubes and are able to get some pellets that way. Not enough really, even with those we steal from their storehouses. I even suspect that the Class One rulers of Resurrection City have sometimes deliberately overlooked this theft, knowing it was the only way to keep the mutants from surging up. But tell me, father, more about the machines which do the farming work."

"They are machines that were developed and used before the great war. So many men were called into service, and so many were killed, large numbers of these machines were built to handle all farm work."

"Are they robots? Do they operate by themselves? Who controls them?"

"I have heard that a certain number of Class Two guards are trained to operate the machines, or at least have electronic control of them. I really know little more."

"One thing more, father. I have never been to the central area. What is there?"

"Everything but the houses where Class Three people like us, live. What we call Resurrection City is really nothing but a small area built on top of the center of the old city. Streets radiate out in thirty or more directions from the central core. At the very middle point is the headquarters where the Class One rulers work and live. Around this are the other buildings—the medical center, the power station, the pellet processing plant, the schools, the shops where materials are fabricated into products."

I thought for a moment. "How many Class One people are there?"

Father's mouth twisted into a wry smile. "No one knows. I have never seen a Class One person, nor has anyone else I've ever heard of. All I know is that certain selected young people at eighteen are operated on. They then become slavishly obedient Class Two members. Somehow they get messages directly into their brains that order them what to do. It is the way the Class One people rule the city."

"Father," I asked, "if I were to walk to the central area in this uniform, would I be challenged?"

"Yes, Rolf. I'm afraid you wouldn't get very far. Most guards go in pairs or in small squads. One alone would be questioned."

"Is there any way I could explore the central area safely?"

Father waved a hand weakly to show that he was confused. "There is no safe way. Possibly you could go as a worker."

"How could I do that?"

He looked at me pensively. "You really are serious about this, aren't you? Willing to risk your life for the mutants!"

He paused and looked over at Gretta who had been listening avidly. "Remember that old tunic I was going to throw away? I think it would fit Rolf."

He turned back to me. "Sleep here tonight. Tomorrow when we leave for work, put on my old tunic and follow along behind us. As long as you keep moving and seem to be going somewhere, you will not be stopped. You can have as much as an hour to walk around during that period when the Class Three workers are coming to their jobs. Then you would have to hide all day. That isn't too hard. A park near the Class One headquarters has bushes and trees which could conceal you. Then, at the end of the day when the workers start going home, you could have another hour to do what further exploring you want. But don't wait too long before coming back here. And be sure you remember the street where we live. Mark it well in your mind when you reach the center. All the streets look alike."

I could see that father was getting more and more tired. I said I thought I had enough information. After kissing Gretta and patting my father's shoulder, I slipped back to my room in the basement.

It seemed strange to me now to be in that tiny place. To think I had spent much of my life there. Better there, of course, than dead. I owed much to my father. As I drifted off to sleep I decided that whatever I did on the following day, I would not bring risk to him and Gretta. How much risk myself I faced, I was almost afraid to guess.

XVII

Dressed in my father's old worn work tunic, I trudged along behind him and Gretta as they made their way to work the next morning. I grieved to see how slowly they moved. They were old.

I watched carefully how they and the others on the street, all headed in the same direction, slouched as they walked. Their eyes were downcast, their expressions all but vacant. I tried to copy their appearance to be as inconspicuious as possible.

I did, however, take quick glances from side to side. The houses themselves were all alike. The walls surrounding them were not alike. Some went only waist high as though the owner of that house became too tired to go higher. Others were two or even three times the height of a man. I recalled what Milo had said about the obsession for walls that dominated the thinking of those in the upper city. Some apparently were more concerned than others.

Slowly as we moved, it was only about a fifteen minute walk to the central area of the city. I could see immediately that this was entirely different than where the homes were located. It had five and six story buildings, some covering large areas. They were of plain construction, without ornamentation, apparently built solely for high functional use. They seemed to be set out in a quad pattern with a still taller, more impressive-looking building in the middle.

Following father's warning, I made a mental note of the street we had come by. I could see other streets with workers coming toward the central work area. I wanted to be sure I knew which one was the right one to return to my father's house at the end of the day.

I watched my father and Gretta as they entered one of the buildings. They never turned to see whether or not I still followed them. I walked on, always with my head down but my eyes darting first to one side and then the other.

Father had said I might have an hour or so for exploration before the last of the workers were in the shops and the streets were empty. Then I would have to hide or face a challenge from the watch guard.

I walked around the inner side of the quad of buildings. One, I could guess by the white-coated men and women entering, was probably the medical center. Men and women in work tunics crowded into most of the other buildings which I had to assume were factories or shops of one kind or another. One building was obviously the power plant. This one I studied out of the corner of my eye as I strolled slowly past it, pretending to limp a little. This, I knew, was the key to the operation of Resurrection City.

The building in the middle drew my attention next. It was not only easily twice as tall as the buildings surrounding it, but it was highly ornate. Even its surface was sheathed with some kind of light-colored shining metal. For the height of five stories there were no windows. Such windows as it had were along the top-five floors. As far as I could see, there was only one entrance, a massive gate-door guarded by four men in the uniforms of the watch guard. It was obvious that protection was the main factor in its construction. There were parks at both front and back. The difference was that the one at the front was open while the one at the back had a high wall surrounding it.

So interested had I become in examining this central building which I assumed was where the Class One rulers lived that I failed to note the passage of time.

Suddenly I realized I was the only person in sight wearing a worker tunic. Furthermore, between me and the open park where father had suggested I hide for the day were standing two of the watch guard men.

All I could do was slip back out of sight around the corner of the tall building. I reached the wall at the rear that enclosed what was probably a private park for the Class One people.

At this moment I saw two more guards swinging along in my direction. I looked up at the wall. It was at least twice my height. Vines covered some of the surface. Would they hold me?

Making a leap upward I grabbed one of the strands. It held. Hand over hand I pulled myself to the top. Even exposed as I was, the guards had not looked my way. I glanced down into the park behind the wall. Right below me was a thick bush. I jumped down, landing awkwardly in a sprawl. Quickly I rolled off the top of the bush and then under it. I waited, hardly daring to breathe. I could hear nothing. Thankfully I had not been spotted. For the moment I was safe.

For an hour I lay under the bush. Then, when I still heard nothing, I squirmed my way out. Crouching, I moved along the lower edge of the wall until I came to a path.

The path, I realized, might be dangerous. I drifted off away from it toward the middle of the park. Never had I seen such dense vegetation—bushes and trees so close to each other that I had trouble making progress through them. I knew what I was doing was foolishly reckless. But here was the best opportunity ever to learn something about the Class One rulers.

I heard a murmer of talk from in front of me. Very carefully I made my way toward the sound. A small opening showed that I had come to a clearing. I peered out.

Two men were seated on a bench directly before me

almost within arm's length. I recoiled in horror. Few of the mutants in Destruction City were as revolting, as horribly repulsive as these two. Completely without clothing, their indescribably hideous bodies were revealed to me in all their obscene frightfulness.

For a moment I was too shocked to accept what I saw. Then it came to me—these men were of the Class One ruling group!

These were the foul descendants of the original survivors of the nuclear war of 1999. Smarter than the rest, they had used the old technology and taken over. Mutants themselves, they had tried to eliminate all other mutants. They were responsible, too, for the cruel system that made mental slaves of the best of the defect-free young people and physical slaves of the rest.

What had Milo said—eliminate the Class One rulers and the biggest obstacle to peace would be removed. I had brought the laser gun I had taken from the guard. But what could one man do?

Holding tight rein to my anger, I listened to the conversation of the two creatures so close in front of me . . .

One was saying—"A beautiful dark-haired one is being treated tomorrow. What is your wish, master?"

The other replied—"I prefer a fair one this time."

"A very choice blond-haired one is scheduled for treatment three days from now. Will you wait for her, master?"

The other laughed, a high-pitched, almost hysterical cackle. "Why wait? It's too easy to have them come to me after the operation. Their brains are no longer theirs. I want this one *before* the operation. I'd like to see how she would react to my appearance. It might be interesting to see how long it would take to break her will so that she would give herself to me of her own volition."

The first one spoke up—"I tried it once. The girl

112

fought back. I had to strangle her to keep from being hurt by her. She was very violent."

"I think I'd like that. Yes, arrange for the blond girl to be brought to me just before she is to be treated. They all seem so happy going to the operation. Let her come to me that way."

"It will be done, master. But what if she attacks you?"

"I can always strangle her, can't I?" the creature laughed as he got up and motioned for his companion to follow him.

I looked with horror at them as they stood before me—loathsome, naked bodies, with hairless oversize heads, noseless, but with huge pendulous lips. Black coarse hair covered much of their bodies. Both had arms that reached almost to the ground. Between the legs of the one called 'master,' dangled what I thought at first was a tail, but was really an overdeveloped phallus. I shuddered in horror.

They moved away down the path. For the moment I was too shaken to do anything. This was the most valuable piece of information I could take back with me—that the rulers themselves were mutants of the most extreme abnormality.

Almost in a daze I returned to my original hiding place. I had to have time to think. I realized, of course, that I now had a powerful weapon to get the Class Three people to side in with the mutants of lower city to overthrow their Class One rulers. Apathetic as the workers were, and crushed in spirit, nevertheless learning how they were being tyrannized by mutant rulers might stir them to action.

All day I waited under my bush. The information I now had was too precious to risk with any further adventuring. My task was to get out safely and go back to Destruction City. There, I would have to form some kind of organization to work with the Class Three workers of upper city, and then develop a plan for destroying the Class One stronghold.

Toward late afternoon I reconnoitered to find a possible way to get over the wall. At one place I saw a tree growing close enough to allow me to climb out on one of its limbs to reach the wall top.

When I estimated that the end of the work day had come and workers would be filling the streets, I climbed the tree. The limb was not as thick as I would have liked. I had never climbed a tree before and I had no idea how much weight the limb would hold. Gingerly I moved out. I was almost to the wall when I heard a slight cracking noise. I jumped just as the tree branch broke. My hands caught at the top of the wall and I pulled myself up.

I peered over. There were scores of workers walking on the street next to the wall. Further on were two guards with their backs to me. Using the vines, I slid down to the ground. Two or three of the workers looked up at me, startled to see me appear as I did. When I merely brushed myself off and slouched over to join the men and women going home, they lost interest.

Now to find the right street. As father had warned, all had exactly the same look. Within minutes, however, I had spotted the landmark I had picked out. Off I went, at the same slow pace of the workers around me.

At my father's house I was uncertain at first, trying to decide which one it was. Fortunately he had stationed Gretta there to watch for me. When I came up, she opened the gate-door and motioned me in.

I had dinner with them. At first I held back from telling them what I had found out. I knew what a shock it would be to them. But before I left, I blurted it all out.

Father was unable to do more than stare at me. Gretta wept, saying that her little girls deserved a better fate than this.

Almost sorry now that I had told them, I could see they were completely crushed. I advised my father to go on doing everything in his usual manner until he heard from me. I also assured them I would use all my influence to protect them.

"What are your plans, Rolf?" my father asked just before I left.

"I don't have any," I said, shaking my head. "There are so many problems. I will try to come back in a few days. All I can advise you now is to go on living as you have."

"But it's so hopeless, Rolf. What is the use of our living? Gretta and I are old. They have no use for workers who are too old to do their tasks. You have no chance to defeat the Class One rulers. The workers will never believe your story that their rulers are mutants. I see only war and death."

"Father," I pleaded, "I am going to the lower city. I am going to try to work out a plan that will avoid war. If the mutants invade the upper city, I hope I can control them so that the takeover is bloodless."

"That's not possible, my son."

"At least that is what I am going to try to do."

But as I climbed down into the lower reaches of Destruction City, I had my doubts too. What was I to do? An invasion now of the upper city would only lead to a bloody, deadly struggle. Would I be able to hold it back until I could develop a plan that had a reasonable chance for success without a lot of killing?

Again I wished that Milo were alive to advise me.

XVIII

If what I had found out on the surface had shocked me, it was nothing to how I reacted to the sight when I reached my space-room.

Marda, her beautiful dark hair spread out fanlike around her head, lay in a pool of blood. Her eyes were glazed. She was barely alive.

I threw myself down on my knees next to her. "What has happened, Marda?"

She tried to smile. "It was Trax," she said, gasping for breath. "He took Witch. I fought him."

"Where are you hurt?"

When she didn't answer me, I pulled up her tunic to see for myself. The gash in her side was gushing blood in regular little spurts. I ran to get a cloth to stem the flow. After I finished bandaging her as best I could, I held her slender body in my arms. I could have loved this girl.

Her eyes opened. "Trax," she whispered, "plans . . . to . . . kill you . . ."

She made a fierce struggle to say more. Her words, when they came, were hardly more than a soft murmur. "Trax . . . invasion . . ."

"When?" I pleaded. "When does Trax plan to attack?"

I waited for her answer. But there was no answer. Marda was dead.

Looking at her lifeless body, I wished I had not destroyed the combination to the vault. A burial next to Milo was what I would have liked for her.

I rose awkwardly to my feet, my eyes half blinded with tears. I took the cover from my bed and put it

117

over her. For several minutes I merely stood and stared unseeing at the floor where her blood still shone in the light of my torch.

What should I do? Go search out Trax and kill him? I patted the laser gun in the pocket of my tunic. One beam from the gun and he would be burned to a cinder.

But what if he or his friends found me first? They knew the passages of Destruction City far better than I. And if I died, who could warn the people of Resurrection City? I owed nothing to them except for father and Gretta. I thought of them being torn to pieces by the mutants, filled with blood lust and hungry to bring vengeance on the people they considered their enemies.

Where really did my loyalties lie? I felt keen sympathy for the mutants. They had suffered much. But the people above, enslaved by the cruel Class One rulers, deserved sympathy too.

I guess what really decided me was my new hatred for Trax and his followers who could kill a lovely girl like Marda. Too, I realized full well that only I could save my father and Gretta.

So, my choice was made for me. I would have to go back up and do what I could to stop the carnage that would come with an invasion by the mutants. How I could do this, I had no idea.

Before leaving my space-room, I looked around. Not only had they taken Witch, but also my gold coin jacket. There was nothing left that I could use. Armed now only with the laser gun and an electric torch, I slipped out into the passageway.

Always I had seen people in these tunnels through the rubble. Now they were deserted. Something had pulled them away. Perhaps a general meeting called by Trax. This would be his great moment. I could even envision him standing before the mutants, wearing my gold jacket, holding up Witch and proclaiming himself the new ruler of Destruction City.

Through empty passageways I made my way back to my secret basement room. The red light was burning. I pushed through into the lower part of the house and up the dark stairs. There were no sounds to greet me. Even as I turned toward the bedroom where my father and Gretta slept, my mind was in a turmoil of frustration. How could I save them? Where could I take them?

The only safe place I could think of was my hidden room. It might protect them for a few days. That might even be enough. After the first violent blood bath, perhaps it would calm down and be safe for them to come out. It was the only place I could think of.

The door was closed. Shielding the light from my handtorch, I opened the door and peered in at the two on the bed. I stepped in and called softly. No answer.

Then, a dull foreboding seized me.

I pulled back the cover and found them clasped in each other's arms, dead. Blood spread out on the bed clothes below them. They had slashed their wrists and died together. Quickly I covered them again.

They were too old, my father had said. Too old to face the troubles ahead, the horror of suffering possible mutilations and tortures by the invading mutants. They had chosen their own way, their own time to die.

I stumbled out into the front room and sank into a chair. One thing this meant. I was now free to carry out any plan I could think of. I could try to warn the Class Three people. I could try to regain control over the mutants many of whom I knew feared Trax. Or I could simply try to save myself:

Sitting there in the dark I tried to review all my obligations and all the avenues of action open to me—

Milo was dead. Marda was dead. Father and Gretta

were dead. There was nothing I could do for any of them.

My two little half sisters, born to my father and Gretta! I doubted if I would be able to find them, or even recognize them.

Ralf! Father had told me that my twin brother was a medic student in the medical center. Almost certainly by now he was in Class Two. Even if I could reach him and warn him, would he believe me?

Elissa! Sitting in the dark as I was, with grief tearing at my heart, it was Elissa I most wanted to save. Marda I could have lived with and been happy with. But it had always been Elissa, the unattainable, whom I had dreamed of. It was Elissa that I loved.

Through the long hours of the night, I sat and tortured myself with wild, impossible plans. By morning, I was as planless as before.

At the first light I went in and made sure that my father and Gretta were covered. Unable to eat anything, I merely took a deep drink of water. When I knew that the workers would be going along the street toward the central section, I slipped out and joined them, leaving the gate-door unlatched. I didn't even look back at the house. I could only look forward now.

Forward to what? My feet moved as slowly and as wearily as the workers in front and behind me on the street. What a stir I could make by shouting out to them to hurry back to their home and cower behind their walls—the mutants were coming!

Or worse yet—what if I screamed the news that their rulers were the most vicious mutants of all!

I plodded along, my head downcast as were those around me. When I reached the central area, I moved with purpose toward the medical center. If I could only see Ralf, there was that slim hope that I could talk with him, warn him about the invasion and suggest we get Elissa and flee together. It wasn't much of a hope, but it was all I had.

Walking slowly past the medical building, I paused for a moment to look up. A tall, blond girl was hurrying toward me. She cried out—"Ralf, why are you wearing that old worker tunic?"

I stopped short. My heart skipped a beat or two. I knew her instantly. It was Elissa . . . beautiful beyond words to describe, with a joyous smile on her fair face, and her hands outstretched towards me.

Speechless, all I could do was take them between my own and press them warmly.

XIX

"Ralf, I'm so glad to see you. Come on in with me to see Lizda's operation. After all she is my best girl friend."

I simply stared, tongue-tied. For all these years I had kept Elissa's image fresh in my mind—a slim, blond, graceful beauty. And here she was, grown up to be a still more lovely slim, blond, graceful beauty.

I started to talk. I had so much to say.

"Come on, Ralf," she said as she grabbed my arm. "Whatever it is, tell me later. We haven't much time."

She skipped merrily along beside me. "Just think, Ralf, only two more days and I'll be eighteen and can have my operation. Then, darling Ralf, I'll be in Class Two like you. And we can be mated. That's what I want more than anything else in life—to be your mate. That's what you want too, isn't it?"

I nodded. If ever I agreed with anything it was that. Even though she had mistaken me for my twin, at least I had this moment, this one moment when she held my arm and turned a face of love to me.

She kept on talking, leaving me to gaze at her. I knew I would have to give my fearsome warning to her soon. But couldn't it wait a minute or two more? This moment would never come again.

"Oh, I wish it were today," she said. "But two days is not too long to wait, is it, darling?"

She paused and looked closely at me. "I still can't see why you're wearing that silly worker tunic. You ought to have your white coat on, like the rest of the student medics. Oh, I suppose you have some dirty laboratory work to do today. Is that it, Ralf?"

Again I nodded weakly.

"Another thing, Ralf, you look as if you've been working too hard. I guess I've been so happy looking forward to my operation that I haven't paid as much attention to you as I should. You look thinner and more tired than usual."

She squeezed my arm. "Just wait until I've had my operation and we've been mated. I'll take good care of you then."

By this time we had entered the medical building. A guard looked quizzically at my worker tunic but apparently identified me as Ralf, as Elissa had done. Leading the way, she put her fingers to her lips. "I promise not to talk any more. I know it's forbidden in the operating theatre. I'm just glad to be able to sit next to you and to know that what is happening to Lizda will be happening to me day after tomorrow."

Before opening the door to what she had referred to as the operating theatre, she gave me a quick kiss on the cheek. Then she said—"I won't be able to stay with you. I promised Lizda I would follow her to the recovery room. As soon as I find out that she is all right, I'm to rush over and tell her father. He'll be so proud of her."

I opened the door. She entered and I followed.

The balcony in the 'operating theatre' was half filled with student medics. None looked up at our entrance. It was a circular room with a pit in the middle. In the pit was a narrow table with a battery of lights directly above the table. It resembled a picture I had seen in one of Milo's books of an old-fashioned hospital operating room. Elissa and I and the student medics were in the balcony that completely encircled the small stage below.

We sat in complete silence. I could even feel the tension build up in Elissa as she gripped my hand in hers.

A cart was pulled in and the unconscious form of a

124

girl was transferred from it to the narrow operating table. Five white-coated men strode in and assembled around the girl.

A covering over her head was removed revealing that her skull had been shaved smooth and clean. It gleamed like a small pink ball under the bright lights.

A tray of instruments was brought over by one of the men. Another man, with calipers and measuring devices, made a half dozen marks at various places on her cranium. A third man picked up a small tool and held the point at one of the marked spots. I could see it was a drill, slowly and carefully boring its way into the brain area. Satisfied that he had reached the proper depth, he withdrew the drill and stepped aside for the fifth man to insert a tiny metal plug.

When this had been repeated five more times, the men stood back and bowed in unison to the student medics in the balcony. They were applauding silently with hands waving in front of their faces. Then the five men walked out.

Three new white-coated men entered. Immediately they began to attach tiny fastenings to the six plugs. This done, they withdrew without bowing.

Following them four white-clad women came in and moved the girl back to the cart. One of them covered the patient's head with a cloth. Before she could push the cart out of the room, I saw that the cloth was already heavily stained with blood. I took a sideways glance at Elissa. She was as white as chalk.

She smiled weakly back at me as we walked slowly to the corridor outside. The operation had clearly shaken her. She squeezed my hand again.

"I'm going down to the recovery room," she said in a rush. "I had no idea the operation was like that. And I'll lose all my hair."

She looked frightened. Then she continued—"As soon as I know how Lizda is, I want to go over and tell her father. He works in the power plant. Could you meet me there in an hour?"

I watched as she moved away from me down the corridor. I too had no idea the operation was like that. And Elissa, beautiful Elissa, with her long blond hair cut off, would have those plugs put into her skull. That, I now realized, was how the Class One rulers kept control over their Class Two leader-slaves. Somehow, out of the old-world technology, they had found a way, possibly through electronic transmitters, to get instant and absolute obedience.

Two days from now Elissa was scheduled to be given this same operation.

Two days from now . . . !

What had the monster in the park said? A blond girl was scheduled in three days, and that was said yesterday. It was Elissa he was talking about. It was Elissa he was going to have brought to him *before* the operation. That would be today.

I looked to see if she were still in sight. I had to warn her. She was gone.

Still standing in a state of confusion in the doorway, I was only dimly aware that the student medics were pushing past me. As the last one passed me, he casually glanced at me. Instantly he stopped and took a second look.

I should have been more prepared for it. After all I knew Ralf was a student medic. I had even hoped to meet him here. And now, almost miraculously, here he was in front of me.

"It can't be," he said. "Is it Rolf, my twin?"

He glanced around nervously and then grabbing my arm, pulled me into a small storage room off the hall. For a moment or two we just stared at each other. Ralf was slightly heavier than I. Otherwise we were still identical. Even with him in his white coat and me in my worker's tunic, we looked exactly alike.

126

I smiled and held out my hand. He took it. For an instant I thought he was going to embrace me.

He was the first to speak. "How are mother and father? I was never allowed to contact them, you know."

"Both are dead. Mother died several years ago. Father died . . . recently." I simply could not tell him that he had killed himself the night before. "And you?" I asked. "How have you been?"

"On my eighteenth birthday, I was honored with the operation that gave me Class Two rating. My hair still hasn't grown out fully. As you can see, I am a student medic. But you, Rolf, what's happened to you? I'm trying to remember. Why didn't you go with me to school?"

"I went to a different school."

"No Class Two rating? I can see by your tunic that you are a worker. What shop are you working in?"

Peering back at him, seeing what I would have become but for my four-toed feet, I wanted with all my heart to save him from the mutant invasion. And Elissa too, even if it meant I would lose her forever to him. He was my twin, my other half. If I couldn't have Elissa, Ralf was the one I would most want to share her life.

"Ralf," I said, "I have something serious to tell you. I am risking my life to come here to warn you. I have learned—no matter how—that the mutants from below are going to invade Resurrection City. Possibly even today. I just talked with Elissa. I didn't get a chance to warn her, but she is to meet me at the power plant in an hour."

"An invasion? That's impossible."

"Ralf, I know it's going to happen. I came here to warn you. More than that, Elissa is in special danger today. If you love her, try to find some way to get her outside the city—today, right now!"

"You're mad, Rolf. The mutants are just animals.

127

They haven't the wits nor the strength to come up out of their holes. I've said for years we ought to kill them all."

My hopes sank. He talked as I would expect a Class Two person to talk. I had only one more argument to use on him.

"Do you know that the Class One rulers are mutants themselves? And that the one they call their 'master' has ordered that Elissa be brought to him today? To be forced to serve him . . . as a slave!"

Ralf glared back at me with shocked expression. "Now I know you are mad, mad! You may mean well in telling me this, but such lies can only come from a twisted mind."

He paused. "I've got a class now I must attend. You said you were meeting Elissa at the power station in an hour. I'll meet the two of you there. Wait for me and I'll prove you are wrong."

As he hurried away to his class, I realized I may have blundered in telling Ralf. As a Class Two man, he was not his own master. Back there in the central head-quarters were creatures who used people like Ralf and Elissa to rule Resurrection City. Would there be any possibility of reasoning with my twin?

I stayed in the storage room, hoping to hide there until the hour had passed and my time for meeting Elissa had arrived. After a time I wandered around the room. In a small closet I found an old white medic coat. It had a tear in one sleeve, but otherwise fit me fairly well. I slipped it on over my worker tunic.

Thinking of the coming meeting with Elissa, I hoped she had not yet been picked by the watch guard to be taken to the headquarters. At least, she had not so far been lobotomized.

Would the hour never end . . . ?

XX

As I left the medical building, wearing the white coat I had found in the closet, one of the guards glanced around at me, smiled and waved.

I could see several small groups of Class Three workers engaged in various tasks in the open park. Each group was watched over by a guard. Evidently the Class One rulers were taking no chances, not even with men and women whose spirit had been crushed by a lifetime of slavery.

At the front of the power plant, I began looking for Elissa. She had said an hour. Every minute could be precious.

Even if I could persuade Elissa to flee with me, I had no idea where to take her. Back to my father's house? The mere thought of having Elissa see those dead bodies, clutched together in their final embrace, was too revolting to consider. Her own parents had long since left the house next door. Could I take her to Destruction City? If Trax had really gained control of the mutants, my life would be forfeit as soon as I appeared. What they would do to Elissa made me shudder. Milo's old domain? Possible. But it led to no permanent solution. Sooner or later we would have to go out for food. Outside the city walls? It was a fearsome thought. No one I knew had ever gone beyond even the inner walls. Yet it was a possibility as a last resort. It would get us away from the known horrors of Resurrection City and Destruction City to the unknown horrors of a land beyond.

I could see Elissa half-running toward me. Her face was aglow with joy. Her arms reached out for me.

"Lizda is fine," she cried happily as she came into my arms for a quick embrace. She stepped back and looked at me. "I'm glad you've gone back to wearing your medic coat. Just think," she said, "I'll be having my own operation day after tomorrow. How soon then, dear Ralf, do you think we can be mated?"

I smiled but said nothing. It was better, I thought, to hold back just a little longer the telling of my fearful warning. I wanted this moment to last.

She grabbed my hand and pulled me toward the entrance to the power plant. Two guards were there. Just as they started to wave us in, two more guards came up.

One of them said to Elissa. "You are wanted at headquarters."

"At headquarters? Now? I've never been there." She seemed flustered.

My hand went into the pocket of my medic coat. I knew what they were here for—to take Elissa to that monster in the control building. I would kill them before I let them take her to that monstrosity.

Quickly she explained her errand, saying she would be back out in two or three minutes. Then, without waiting for their approval, she seized my hand impulsively and dashed into the building with me next to her.

"I've just got to tell Lizda's father the good news," she said, hurrying a step or two in front of me. At a door, guarded by two more of the watch guard, she halted for a moment and explained her mission. They motioned us in.

It was the control room. Along two walls were banks of switches, dials, levers, meters, control of all types. This was the vulnerable heart of the power facility by which the ruling mutants controlled all Class Two men and women.

I was torn with a moment of indecision. This was my golden opportunity to deal a death blow to Class One rule over the city. Aiming my laser gun at the row of controls would burn them out. At the same time it would make it easier for the mutants of the lower city to take over.

Elissa had hurried over to talk excitedly to a man at one of the controls. I could see two guards standing at a window at the far end of the room. They seemed excited at what they were looking at. One of them suddenly turned and headed at a run for the door. The other stayed where he was, still looking out. I had a feeling that the mutants had started their invasion and that was what he was watching.

Thinking of those two guards waiting outside to take Elissa to 'headquarters,' I hesitated no longer. I slipped out of sight of the guard and crouched behind a control cabinet. I pulled out my laser gun and aimed it at the nearest line of switches and dials. I had no idea which ones would stop the flow of power.

Disregarding the Class Two people in the room, including the one remaining guard, I directed the beam from my gun along the length of one row of controls and then on to the other side.

"Ralf!" I could hear Elissa scream at me. "What are you going?"

All about us the room hissed and crackled with violent electric shorts. Then came explosions that rocked the whole building.

The Class Two people in the room were on their knees holding their heads and screaming in pain. Once the electrical connection was broken apparently they had no minds of their own.

I seized Elissa by the hand and rushed her out into the corridor. Glancing back I could see the control room was an inferno, with flashes and fires springing up everywhere. The guards in the hallway were on their knees, pounding frantically at their heads. I picked up their laser guns.

Belatedly I felt a rush of pity for the helpless victims of my act. But now I faced a real problem—how to save Elissa!

I could see she was stunned by what was happening. She followed me blindly as I led the way outside. The four guards at the entrance were groveling in pain on the ground.

Across in the park was a milling around of people—Class Three workers shocked by the collapse of their guards. Some, I saw, were beginning to try to protect themselves against the horde of mutants pouring into the square from two sides.

Quickly I gathered up the laser guns from the four guards writhing at our feet. I might need as many as I could get. And I didn't want them to fall into the hands of the mutants. Then I stripped off the medic coat and threw it aside.

Ralf! He was to meet us at this spot. I tried to see him in the score or more of Class Two men rolling in agony on the ground near us. Suddenly I spotted him.

He had twisted over on his side and was looking up at me. It was a look of sheer agony. Unable to speak, he made a motion toward Elissa and then pointed away from the battle that was taking place in the park. The message he gave me was unmistakable. I was to save Elissa.

She had been hanging onto my arm, only half conscious of what was happening around us. She had not seen Ralf.

A howl of rage came from a new mob of mutants as they entered the park from a different direction. A part of them headed towards us.

I looked again at Ralf. His eyes, filled with pain as they were, nevertheless pleaded with me to save Elissa.

My brother! My twin! My other half! As much as I would have given my own life to save him, I knew there was no chance.

"We'll have to run for it," I yelled at Elissa. I grabbed her arm.

I had noted that the mutant invasion had come from only three sides of the quadrangle. I headed the fourth way. When we reached the street leading to my father's house, I was thankful I had marked it well the first time.

Elissa seemed to be in better control of herself. Without asking me where or why we were running, she jogged along beside me.

At my father's house, I was glad I had left the gate-door unlatched. We had seen only a few bewildered Class Three people in our hurry to reach what I hoped would be at least a temporary haven of safety. I could hear sounds of explosions from behind us.

After we had gone through the gate-door, I locked it behind us. At the house I hurried Elissa through, down the stairs and into my old secret room.

I told her to stay quietly there while I got some supplies upstairs. I deliberately avoided going into my father's bedroom. In five minutes I was back with one of Gretta's warm worker tunics for Elissa and a pair of heavy worker shoes for her. Also I had a bag of food pellets and another bag of fresh vegetables which could be eaten raw. Several spare batteries for my electric torches completed my stock of supplies, together with the laser guns I had picked up from the fallen guards, six altogether.

When I returned, Elissa met me with a questioning expression. "What is happening, Ralf? Why did you bring me here? Where are we?"

"Elissa," I said, "you'll have to trust me. When we have time, I'll explain it, although I'm not sure I understand it all either."

"What do we do now, Ralf? We can't stay here."

"We're not going to."

I went over to the corner of the small room and lifted

the cover from the hole I had dug so many years before. I pointed. "We are going down there."

"Why, Ralf? What are we running from?"

"We're running from certain death, Elissa. The mutants are taking over Resurrection City."

She shook her head as though unable to believe what I was telling her. "But if we go down there, aren't we going directly into where they live?"

"Not exactly. You'll just have to trust me. I'm doing the only thing I know to save us."

She came up and put her arms around me. Her body was trembling. "I do trust you, Ralf. I'll do whatever you say."

Although I could have descended in the dark, I directed my light to show Elissa each step of the way down. At the bottom, I moved with assurance to Milo's old area in the bank rooms. The electric light was out. If nothing else, this would have proved to me that I had really knocked out the power system.

"We'll stay here tonight," I said. "We're perfectly safe here. Our greatest danger will be tomorrow. We should try to get a good sleep tonight."

I showed her my old sleeping pad which I had used when I stayed with Milo. After drinking from the small extra supply of water I had brought with me, I kissed her good night. For a long time she clung to me frantically.

"I do trust you, Ralf. But you seem so different here. More determined, somehow."

"Sleep well," I murmured into her ear as I tucked the cover over her.

I went back to the room where Milo had stored his collection of books. Although the place was completely without light, I could have gone to the shelves and picked out any one of them. I had read and reread them all. I knew them as friends and companions through all those years after I was doomed as a child of six to stay hidden from the cruel Class One rulers.

How successful had been the invasion? Were the mutants in control? Were they killing all Class Three people? Were they to be the new masters of the city, making the worker class serve them as slaves?

I thought of our own plight. To take Elissa along the passageways through Destruction City would be too perilous. At first sight of us, Trax and his men would tear us apart. My laser guns would be little use against a mob of them. And anyway, I had had enough of killing.

As a boy in those long years with Milo, I had made many exploration trips through the rubble areas back of Milo's room. No mutants lived there. The air was not good enough. While I had never found a real exit to the outside, there were two or three places that I remembered as being fairly promising.

Even as I thought of those possible exits to the outer world, I sensed that some inner hunger in me was pulling me that way. Milo had spoken of the restricting obsession for physical and mental walls in both the upper and lower cities, walls separating people, stultifying their minds, making them easily victim to slavery and fear and hatred. I wanted no further part of that kind of life.

As I drifted off to sleep, my thoughts were on what the world beyond the walls might be like. The books in Milo's collection had pictures of forests and vast stretches of grass prairies, of mountains and rivers and deserts. Which of these would we find if I could discover a way out?

And the people out there—would they be savages waiting to tear us apart? Or would they have the good will and tolerance that Milo had always set as the ideal?

135

XXI

When I awoke Elissa the next morning, she clutched at my hand. "It's so dark," she said. "I'm afraid."

I switched on my torch and showed her where she was.

"Then it isn't all a bad dream," she murmured.

She slid sideways off the sleeping pad and stood up. She had taken off her tunic and was wearing only a light undergarment. I couldn't help gazing at her.

When I tried to turn on the water in the wash room Milo had built, nothing happened . . . another result of the power failure. This was all the more reason why we had to leave as quickly as possible. The water I had brought with me wou'd last us only a day. Any hope I had of holing up in Milo's rooms until the worst of the trouble was over was now gone.

She looked at me, seeing the consternation on my face. "Please, Ralf, tell me what is happening. How did you know to come here? From the way you act, you've been here before. Have you?"

"Yes, Elissa, I've been here before. I had thought it might be a refuge for us until we found out if it was safe to go back to the upper city. But we have no water. Now we have only one course, and that's to go out beyond the walls."

"Beyond the walls?" she cried in horror. "But there's only wilderness out there, with wild animals. You can't mean it."

"Again I have to ask you to trust me, Elissa. I honestly believe it is our only way to safety."

"Safety? How can you say that?"

I touched her arm lightly. "There is no safety for us

in either the upper or lower city. We have no other choice. We've been told it's a wilderness out there. We've been told it is full of wild beasts. But I have never talked with anyone who has ever been there. We've got to take this chance, Elissa. It's our only hope."

She put on her over-tunic and stood before me. I could see she was disheartened and confused. I put my arms around her and held her close.

"I love you, Elissa," I murmured.

She sobbed. "That's the only thing that matters. And I love you too, Ralf."

My heart sank. There had been few opportunities before to tell her in the flight that I was not Ralf but his twin Rolf. I wanted now to blurt out the truth. And yet something told me to hold back a little longer. While she still thought of me as her promised mate, Ralf, she would have faith in me and follow. In the dangers I feared were ahead of us, I desperately needed to have her willing aid and cooperation. I tried not to think how she would react to the news that I was not Ralf.

"I think we should start as soon as possible," I said, my arms still holding her tightly to me.

"Everything is so strange, so frightening," she said, "but I'm ready."

I turned the beam of my light around the room. Would I ever see it again? Not likely. And Milo— would his bones be found at some long distant future date when men dug down and broke into the vault where I had buried him?

With that glance I put all my past behind me. My father and mother and Gretta. Milo. Marda. Ralf. All were dead. All that was gone.

"Come," I said as I swung my two bags of supplies over my shoulder. I led Elissa along the most promising of the paths that I had explored as a boy. When we came to a place where I stopped before, I stood for a moment in uncertainty. This was as far as I had gone. There was a branching here with no particular advantage to either.

I chose the left branch because it seemed slightly less filled with rubble than the other. For an hour we pushed our way along, pulling aside debris that often blocked our way. It was slow going. My impression was that it was a passage cleared many years before and abandoned

While our progress was slow, it was steady. Elissa made no complaint as we struggled to overcome one obstacle after another, although I could see she was tiring.

Suddenly I held up my hand to hold her back. I turned off my light.

Ahead I could hear the murmur of voices. The path must have taken us right back into the mutant area. The sensible thing would be to turn back and retrace our steps. But I wanted to know what had happened on the surface. I might not have another chance to learn.

I whispered to Elissa to stay quietly where she was. I said I would be back as soon as I could—possibly in only a few minutes.

Leaving her in the dark, I felt my way the few more steps to a place where oddly enough I could look out and down on a small gathering of mutants. Facing the band, with his back to me, was Trax. He was wearing my gold coin jacket. And he was holding Witch high over his head.

"Remember," he shouted, "I am the Master of Witch and rule now not only in Destruction City but in Resurrection City. We are winning. The battle is nearly over. Even now our people are massacring all who live in the upper city who won't bow to us and to our rule."

He halted, his anger apparent even in the set of his shoulders so close below my hiding place.

"Vengeance is ours!" he screamed. "But now—you who have held back, you too can be the target of our vengeance. Only those who have shared in the invasion will be permitted to enjoy the riches of Resurrection City. That is why I left the battle to come down here to rout out every last one of you. We need you all to finish the fight. The watch guard and all the Class Two people were paralyzed when the power went off. When we entered the central Class One headquarters, all we found were about thirty mutants, probably slaves of the rulers. When they resisted us, we killed them all. We need you all to help search for the rulers and to help us control the Class Three people."

"Follow me!" he shouted, "or face death when I return."

Something in me exploded. Perhaps it was thought of the slaughter this vicious mutant was inflicting on the innocent Class Three people above. More likely it was remembrance of Marda lying in a pool of blood, struck down by this madman.

What I did then was foolhardy, crazy, insane. And yet I had to do it.

I reached through the opening in front of me, too small a hole to crawl through, but big enough to reach out and seize Witch from Trax's upraised hand.

Then, in a strong voice of authority, from my hidden place above them, I cried out— "You, Trax, are not the Master of Witch. You are a monster who only deserves to die."

Through the tiny opening I could see the mutants fall on their knees in awe at my voice seemingly coming from nowhere. Trax swung around, his face a mask of surprise and fear. I saw him fumbling at his tunic for his laser gun.

I thought of Elissa back of me in the dark passageway. One shot from the gun Trax was pulling out and she would be alone and terrified.

140

No more killing I had promised myself. But here I could see it was kill or be killed. Carefully I raised my gun even as Trax was leveling his in the direction my voice had come from. I pressed the control button.

I didn't wait to see him disintegrate. Instead I hurried back to where I had left Elissa. The mutants, I felt, would be too stunned to make any effort to follow us. I switched on my torch and directed the beam at Witch. She lay quietly in my hand, silent and limp. She was dead.

Even though she was dead, Trax had tried to use her. I put down the furry little body and motioned to Elissa that we were going to retrace our path.

If she had asked me what had happened, I could not have told her. I was too choked up. No more killings, I had said. And yet I had just killed a man.

At the cross passage, this time we took the route to the right. My confidence in finding a way out was gradually slipping from me. How long could we wander in this ruined area of the old city? How long indeed?

XXII

All the rest of that day we struggled though the tangled remains of what had once been a thriving city of two million people. As we went, my respect for Elissa's spunk and courage increased with every bit of progress we could make.

This was all new to her. She was frightened. And even though the young people like Elissa who were scheduled for elevation to Class Two rating had the best of physical training, I knew she was not prepared for anything as strenuous as this.

Sometimes we found accidental openings in the piles of rubble. Often they led nowhere and we had to retrace our steps. At other times I would have her rest while I cut through obstacles with one of my laser guns. How thankful I was that I had gathered up a number of them. Already I had used up the charges in two of them.

When I saw that Elissa could go no further, I called a halt. We were faced with another big cutting job and I felt it would be better if we tackled it after a sleep.

"We'll stay here tonight," I said. Elissa slid down to her knees in utter exhaustion. When I handed her a food pellet, she started to push it away, then changed her mind. I let her have what little water was left.

The air here was cool but not cold. I knew that, weary as we were, we would be chilled in the night unless we kept each other warm. I wanted to hold her close to protect her and shield her. I wondered if I dared.

Elissa solved the problem by stretching out full

length and beckoning to me. "I'm so tired and scared, Ralf, my love. I want your arms around me."

I switched off the light and lay down next to her. Her back was to me. My left arm went around and my hand tentatively slid across her left breast. She brought a hand up to make sure I stayed there.

"I'm not frightened now," she whispered as we brought our bodies together, my knees under the backs of her thighs.

I thought it would be impossible for me to go to sleep with her in my arms. A dream come true. But sleep came quickly. It seemed like only minutes later when I awoke. During the night we had turned and Elissa was at my back, her body up against mine. I opened my eyes.

I was surprised to note how light it was. I looked up. The layers of rubble over our heads was the thinnest I had ever seen. Daylight came through the many openings.

Here was hope! I reasoned that the rubble would be less thick the further out from the center we went. Perhaps we were near the edge.

I stood up and looked down at the still sleeping girl. She moaned softly and reached out with her hands. When she didn't find me, her eyes opened in shocked surprise.

"Time for breakfast," I said as I knelt beside her and kissed her cheek.

"Oh, Ralf, for a moment I thought you had gone and left me."

For answer I gave her a warm hug.

"I feel stiff and lame all over," she said as she struggled to her feet.

I pointed to the light filtering in from overhead. "It's a bright sunny day. But more important, I really feel we're near the end of our crawl through the ruins. It's

144

a good thing too, because we haven't any water left. That means we've got to find a way out today."

In the new light, I had noticed ahead and to the left a large metallic object. I decided to investigate. It took us a good half hour to reach it. Even then I wasn't sure it was worth the effort. It was a huge pipe fully the height of a man in diameter. It seemed to make a slight grade to the right. The interesting thing was that its top seemed to be fairly free of debris.

I climbed up and pulled Elissa after me. For another half hour we wormed our way, crawling on hands and knees in a straddle along the top. Then this relatively easy passage stopped with a break in the pipe. It had been ruptured and twisted so that there was an opening. Beyond the break was a veritable tangle of steel beams and piles of stone. The pipe, however, seemed to pass under this formidable obstacle.

I slid down from the pipe and looked in. It had a foul odor and slime covered the bottom ankle deep. I tried to remember anything I may have read about pipes like this. It was probably a sewer in that long dead city.

"What a bad smell," Elissa said as she stood next to me while I peered into the opening.

"A bad smell is unpleasant but it won't kill us. This pipe may be our salvation. My guess is that it was a sewer and it goes to the outside. Are you game, Elissa, to try it with me?"

For answer she took a step in. Instantly she backed out, holding her nose. "Do we have to?" she cried.

"Not only does it offer the easiest way out, it may be the only way out for us." I pointed at the jungle of debris ahead of us. "It would be impossible for us to cut our way through all that."

"All right, Ralf. But kiss me first before I get all dirtied up in this slime."

Her lips on mine was the most wonderful feeling

I had ever had. Tired as I was, I could have fought whole mobs of mutants or squads of the watch guard to protect her. But as we broke apart, I had a piercing thought—would she have kissed me if she knew I was Rolf, a mutant? More than ever, I was decided to keep my secret as long as possible.

"Come, my dear," I said as I took her hand. I directed my torch ahead. All I could see was the hollow inside of the pipe with the layer of sludge at the bottom.

For almost an hour we pushed our way through the muck which at times reached over our knees. Going was slow and hard, but not as slow or hard as the struggle of the day before when we had the rubble to contend with. At length we saw a light ahead. When we reached it, I saw that it was another rupture in the pipe. Beyond the break the pipe went off at a slight turn. Cautiously I peered out of the open break. I took a second look. We were on the surface. There was no rubble here at all.

I lowered myself to the ground and helped Elissa down. A short distance ahead of us was the main inner wall of the city from the looks of it. It was fully as high as the height of four men. What were the old measuring symbols used in Milo's books? The wall would be something like seven meters high, or about twenty four feet.

Another obstacle! How could we solve this one?

To top everything off, Elissa started to laugh hysterically. She was pointing at me. I looked down. My tunic was covered with green slime. My arms and legs and even my face was caked with the muck we had gone through in the pipe.

Then, realizing she was in no better condition, Elissa began to cry. I let her hold her head on my shoulder while I patted her back. She had gone through a lot in the past day or two. The emotional let-down was quite natural. But after a few minutes she wiped her dirt-covered face and gave a wan smile.

"Where to now, Ralf?"

I pointed ahead. "Somehow we have to get through or over that wall if we hope to get outside the city area. Our only chance is to find a gate-door."

Oddly enough that's exactly what we found—a gate-door. It was partly open as though the mechanism had stopped either while it was opening or closing. I quickly guessed why. With his hands still clutched at his head, the body of a dead watch guard was sprawled out in the opening. When the power stopped, the gate's electrical control halted. And what happened to the soldier was what must have happened to all Class Two persons. Torture for a few minutes. Then when they could stand the pain no longer, they had died.

I shuddered at thought of Ralf suffering this fate.

I pulled Elissa through the gate, trying to get her past the dead guard as rapidly as possible.

On the other side of the gate, we found ourselves in a low, one-story building that was part of the wall. The room we were in had a solid bank of thick glass windows facing out from the wall. Along the window area was a control board, somewhat like the one in the power plant. On the floor next to the board were three dead guards, still lying where they had died, their hands clutching their heads.

After picking up their laser guns, I looked out through the windows. There, before us, almost as far as I could see, were tilled fields. Tractor-like machines stood idle at various places. With no one controlling their motions, they were as dead as the men at our feet.

It was in these fields food was grown to be processed into the food pellets that were the basis for life in Resurrection City. I had heard vague stories about this. No one I had ever talked with had ever seen these fields.

Apparently the Class One rulers trusted only their Class Two guard-slaves to direct the robotic machines.

Searching around in the building I found a bottle of water. It contained just enough for us to have one good drink each.

At the end of the building I found a small exit door. Unlike the gate, it was not electronically controlled. I opened it and we stepped out onto the soft loam of the field.

Refreshed with the water, and relieved not to be fighting our way through rubble or muck, we strode along. Except that I was inwardly terrified at the possible dangers facing us ahead when we reached the 'wilderness' beyond the outer wall, I would have liked to have lifted my face to the open sky and sang for joy.

We passed several of the robot machines. They had stopped whatever they were doing in mid-motion. Undoubtedly they were products of the old technology, saved from the wreckage and brought into use by the Class One rulers of Resurrection City.

For more than an hour we walked along, resting when we wanted. We went through fields of various kinds of growing things, most of which I was familiar with from our own little garden patch at home. Ahead was a solid row of trees. The only trees I had ever seen were the scrawny ones in the two parks of the upper city. These were huge things, towering up and up.

As we came to them, I realized the row of trees was really a cover for the wall behind. This would be what Milo had hinted at as the outer wall—beyond which lay the great mysterious wilderness.

After exploring each way along the base of the wall for about an hour, I came to the conclusion that there were no gates or openings. All we found of importance was an irrigation ditch running parallel to the wall about fifty paces from it. It was filled with pure running water and we both took long drinks.

I looked up at the wondrous trees. I remembered

how I had escaped from the park back of the Class One headquarters. Could I do here what I did there? Here the trees were much taller. And the wall was fully twice as high.

Telling Elissa to stay below, I began to climb a tree that had sturdy-looking limbs that reached almost to the top of the wall. As far as I was able to see it was the only tree with the potential for reaching the wall top. I climbed out on the limb and looked across. It would take a strong jump. But I felt it could be done.

I went down and told Elissa what I planned for us to do and that it involved some danger. She smiled bravely.

It was already late in the afternoon. To try to cross the wall and face whatever was on the other side at night seemed like needless risk. I made up a bed of leaves and brush under one of the spreading trees.

Then Elissa made a suggestion. "I feel filthy. Why don't we bathe in the stream and try to wash the worst of the mud off our clothes?"

Without waiting for an answer, she slipped off her tunic and out of all but a tight-fitting undergarment. Then she ran to the irrigation ditch and waded in to thigh depth.

I gazed at her all-but nude body with delight—the curved-in slender waist, the gently rounded hips and thighs, the firm high breasts—as she splashed water over herself. The girl of six was now a woman of eighteen, a dream creature more alluring, more exciting than even my most ardent visions had imagined.

She motioned for me to come in with her. I stripped off my things except for the small kilt that all men wore, and plunged in beside her. We cupped water in our hands and playfully tossed it at each other, laughing all the while. We rubbed the caked mud off our arms and legs. Never had I been happier. My heart sang with joy as we frolicked.

I gathered up our clothes. By rubbing and pounding them, I was able to get rid of the worst of the filth we had accumulated in the sewer duct. Before I was finished

149

with the task, Elissa ran from the water and hurried to the bower I had arranged for our night's sleep.

After wringing out the garments as best I could, I spread them out on the ground in the sun which was still an hour or so short of setting.

Suddenly self-conscious, I strode over to look down on her as she lay waiting for me. She was smiling, a smile of welcome.

"Ralf," she said softly as she looked up at me, "do you realize that today is my eighteenth birthday? Today is the day I was scheduled to have my operation. Then, with a Class Two rating, I would be eligible to be your mate."

Hearing her say these things now, and looking down at her lying there, her lovely body still glistening with beads of water, I realized what a terrible mistake I had made in not telling her earlier that I was not Ralf, her promised one, but Rolf, the mutant.

Her voice went—

"Here we are, my love, really together. Tomorrow—who knows what dangers we may be facing. Tonight we have each other. I love you, Ralf. Stay with me. Love me. Do you love me as much as I love you?"

I stumbled for words. "Elissa," I mumbled, "I love you more than life itself." Then I hesitated. Now, if ever, I had to tell her. Where were the words that would explain without shocking her, without turning her love into hate?

I stood mute next to her as she turned toward me.

"Oh, Ralf!" she cried out happily as she reached out for me.

Then, suddenly, she froze. Her gaze had become transfixed.

I glanced down. My four-toed feet! She was staring at them, her look one of horror.

For a moment she could not speak. Then she cried out the dread words—"You are a mutant! You are not Ralf!"

PART THREE

BEYOND THE WALLS

XXIII

The next morning found Elissa wan and glassy-eyed. All night I had heard her turn and toss on the other side of the shelter I had originally provided for the two of us.

She wouldn't speak to me, or even look at me. When I handed her a food pellet, she took it listlessly. When I brought her a drink of water, she swallowed it indifferently. Once she got up and started to walk back toward Resurrection City. I ran over and grabbed her before she reached the irrigation ditch. She tried to squirm out of my grasp as I brought her back.

Why had I not thought to hide my feet! Only a day more and we would have been across the wall and into whatever lay beyond. Now, with her hating me and uncooperative, I didn't know what would happen.

I plumped her down next to our shelter and sat opposite her. Her eyes were fixed on the ground. Her lips were compressed tightly.

"Elissa, whatever you may think of me, I love you. Everything I have done has been out of love for you. I have always loved you since Ralf and I watched you play in your yard next to ours.

"You are shocked that I am Rolf and not Ralf. What is the great difference? He had five toes on each foot. I have four. That is all the difference. Is it so important?

"I'm not even sure I am a mutant. Small physical defects like mine were often ignored in the old days before the war. I've read books on the subject—old books written by scientists back in the twentieth century—and many of them agree that such minor defects do not necessarily carry on to the next generation. And yet, Elissa, I was branded as a mutant, one to be killed as soon as born. I lived in that secret room in my father's basement . . . like an animal . . . not much better than the mutants of Destruction City.

"And for what? For the glory and power of a few Class One rulers! Not for the good of the people. They were only slaves. And the most victimized of the slaves were those in Class Two.

"Elissa, listen to me and wake up to what I saved you from. There is only death and slavery back in the city.

"There is something I must tell you, Elissa. I told it to Ralf and he wouldn't believe it. I don't suppose you will either. What I want to tell you is the bitterest truth of all—the Class One rulers you served were mutants themselves."

At that, Elissa looked up.

"Not only that, Elissa my love, but you must accept the fact that Ralf is dead. I saw him as he lay dying."

"You lie," she said coldly. "As you have lied ever since I first saw you. Leave me alone."

I stood up. "No, Elissa, I will not leave you alone. You are going with me over the wall. Now get up! Right now!"

When she didn't move, I seized one wrist and pulled her to her feet. She turned toward the stream and would have rushed over and thrown herself in. I put my arms around her and held her back.

"You are being stubborn and foolish, my darling," I pleaded.

I half pulled her over to the tree I had spotted the day before. Then, although she refused to let me touch her, she did manage to climb up to the limb that stretched out toward the top of the wall.

I sidled carefully to the end of the branch, gauged the distance, and leaped. As quickly as I regained my balance, I turned and held out my arms for her to follow me.

My heart almost stopped a beat. She was not looking

154

at me but at the ground below. Was she so filled with despair that she really would deliberately fall and kill herself?

"Elissa!" I called out sharply. "It's just a short jump. I'll catch you."

I could see indecision in her face. Then, tears rolling down her cheeks, she leaped. Whether she intended to fall to the ground below or not, her effort was just short of reaching the top of the wall. I reached out as far as I could and grabbed one flailing arm. Unbalanced as it made me, I sank to my knees with my toes hooked over the outer edge of the wall.

For a moment or two she swung in an arc below me. Then, pulling with all my strength, I gradually worked her up to the top alongside me. Panting with exertion and terrified at what she had apparently tried to do, I held her quivering body.

"It's all right now, Elissa my love," I said as I stroked her tear-stained cheek.

After a time, still holding her limp hand, I stood up and peered off beyond the wall. A wilderness? Yes, it was made up of a dense forest, dark and forbidding.

How to get to the ground was now my new problem. The top of the wall was wide enough to walk on with reasonable safety. But would Elissa be steady enough for it?

I pulled her to her feet and set her in front of me, my arms holding her from making any moves to either side. For several minutes we walked slowly that way, my chest tight up against her back, half pushing her ahead of me.

I could see no way to get down. No trees grew close enough to the wall to be of any use. No bushes were at the base to cushion a jump. I was beginning to lose heart when I saw it—a ladder!

The ladder was sturdy and looked well made. It

stood against the outer wall, an open invitation to leave the safety of the wall and descend into the forest.

A trap? That couldn't be. No one from Resurrection City ever tried to cross the two walls. No, more likely it was set there for use by the forest-dwellers. Probably they used it to cross over and steal the food being grown in the fields.

That meant there were people here. What kind of people? Savages who would kill on sight, or make slaves of us? Nothing Milo had told me, or anything I had read, gave me any idea what to expect.

Standing as we were on the wall's top, we were open targets. Were we being watched now? Were they waiting for us to come down the ladder so they could seize us?

I knew I really had no choice of action. Slowly I worked around so that Elissa was protected by my body as we descended the ladder. At the bottom I was both relieved and yet filled with concern. Best to get away from that open space in front of the wall as quickly as possible. At a half-stumbling run, I pulled Elissa into the shelter of the forest.

Our emotions drained from us, we sank to the thick matting of leaves and ferns and twigs that constituted the forest floor. I sat and thought. I was sure now that there were humans here. We would have to proceed carefully. If and when we found the forest people, I wanted to be able to see them first. I didn't like the idea of being surprised.

I had thought Elissa foolish for trying to go back to Resurrection City. Maybe I was the foolish one for even attempting to escape into this unknown land.

I glanced over at Elissa. She was shaking with soundless sobs. I touched her arm to comfort her. She flinched and drew away from me.

"Come, Elissa. We can't stay here."

Slowly and awkwardly she got to her feet. Her joyous spirit was completely gone. She merely stood waiting

156

to follow in whatever direction I took, without a will of her own, dull and submissive.

I led the way through the brush at right angles away from the wall. Within two minutes it was lost to our sight. I looked around. The vastness and majesty of the trees were overwhelming to my senses. Then I remembered something. In my bag was the compass my father had given me long ago. He had said then that it might not work in the rubble of the old city, but that out in the open it would always point north.

I dug it out. With it in my hand, I estimated that if we went west by the compass, we would be going away from the wall. At least we would not be wandering around in circles.

For about two hours we moved steadily forward. Although fallen trees sometimes offered obstacles in our path, it was not nearly as difficult as the struggle we had had to force our way through the ruins of the old city.

Just as I was about to call a rest, I heard a gurgle of water falling ahead. A moment later we burst out on a stream with a small waterfall. At that same instant I saw a path—a human-made path—leading down to it. Seizing Elissa by the arm, I pulled her back with me out of sight in the bushes.

XXIV

For some time we huddled down among the bushes. This was, I realized, an opportunity to find out what the forest people might be like. Undoubtedly this little waterfall was visited by them for fresh water or for bathing. I settled back. Elissa had curled herself into a small ball and had gone to sleep.

I too must have dozed, for I awoke with a start. I could hear voices. They came from next to the waterfall. Taking care not to put my weight on anything that would snap, I stood half erect and looked out.

Two women were bathing under the fall of the water. They were naked. They were just too far away for me to hear what they were saying to each other. Their backs were to me. Then they turned.

Both women were mutants!

One had two extra, very short arms extending from below her shoulders. The other had three breasts and still another large growth on her side.

"Pretty, aren't they?" came a deep voice from behind me.

I jerked around in surprise. Standing over us were three men—giants almost. At least they were the tallest, biggest men I had ever seen, taller and heavier than I. Their expressions were stern.

"Don't try to pull out a gun," the one in the middle said.

Awakened by the talk, Elissa sat up. She crawled over to me and clung to my hand. Then realizing what she had done, she pulled herself away from me and stood up.

"We have been following you ever since you and your woman came down our ladder at the wall," the man said. "We wanted to find out what you were up to. Our settlement is not far from here. You will come with us. But first I must ask you to give us any weapons you may have."

I had brought six laser guns with me. Five I had put in the pockets of my tunic. These I gave to the man. The sixth gun was buried among the food pellets I had put into the bag. I hoped to keep that one at least. But no—one of the other men reached out and took the bag from me.

The man motioned for me to proceed toward the waterfall. The two mutant women were still there. They looked up as we appeared, smiled at the men, and completely unabashed by their nakedness kept on with their bathing.

I peered around quickly at the three men. They were not mutants. If ever I had seen perfect physical specimens, these were the ones.

For several minutes we made our way along what appeared to be a well-traveled foot path. Finally I could hear a frightening sound ahead, and a big, black animal came bounding toward us. I stopped short at sight of the strange beast. Elissa, who had been a step in front of me, turned and pressed herself up against me. I waited for the men to do something to defend us. Instead, the lead man merely leaned over as the creature came running up and ran his hand across its head and behind its ears.

The leader of the group saw our terror. He laughed. "Have you never seen a dog before? He's a pet. He wouldn't harm you. See, he's coming to sniff you. When he's done that, pat his head. Then he'll know you next time."

Elissa huddled behind me as I reached over and touched the beast's head, I looked at its eyes. They were liquid pools of friendliness. I stooped down and put my arms around its big, black, warm body. It gave a short bark of pleasure. A moment later it was bounding joyously ahead of us up the path.

Around another turn and we came to a large open space. There were about thirty crude log cabins in the area. Several more dogs and a dozen or more children came running up. There were grown people too. But I had little opportunity to observe them as our captors hurried us into the largest of the cabins.

This building consisted of one large room with the most primitive of hand-made chairs and a table as the only furniture. Elissa and I were given seats at the end of the room furthest from the one doorway.

So far we had been treated well except for their taking my bag of supplies. My hope began to climb that perhaps these were not the savages I had feared might be living in the forest. I smiled reassuringly at Elissa. She looked away.

Following us into the building were about forty people—old, middle aged, young, men and women. At least half of them had visible evidence of being mutants.

The man who had captured us sat down in front of us. "My name is Fletcher, the arrow-maker. For this year and next I am what we call chief in the community. I tell you this so you'll know I have the authority to question you. First what are your names?"

I told him.

"Why do you come here?"

I replied we were fleeing for our lives.

"From Slave City?"

When I looked up in surprise at his calling it that, he said, "That's how we know it." He glanced around at the others who nodded that they agreed. "We have always called it Slave City. My grandfather, over fifty years ago, escaped from there. He was not what they call a mutant, but my grandmother was. He brought her here. While he was still alive he told us many stories about life in the city. That was when they were finishing construction of the double walls. He and grandmother were the very last to get out. How were you able to leave? No one in fifty years has ever crossed the outer wall even though we have left ladders at several points along its length."

Briefly I told the group of what had happened in Resurrection City and Destruction City . . . the cruel Class One mutant rulers . . . the controlled Class Two leader-slaves . . . the Class Three worker-slaves . . . the mutant city in the rubble below the old city . . . the mutant invasion . . . my destruction of the power plant . . . our struggle to escape.

"I don't understand one thing," Fletcher broke in. "If the Class One rulers were mutants themselves, why did they persecute the other mutants?"

I thought for a moment. "I had only one chance to see any Class One man, two of them. Perhaps they feared the mutants in the lower city would come up out of their burrows and take over the city. They knew they could control the Class Two people through electronic means. By crushing the spirit of the Class Three workers, they had a slave population serving them. All I can say is that apparently for seventy years, a relatively small nucleous of technically trained mutants and their descendants have ruled what you call Slave City. A very appropriate name too. Much more appropriate than Resurrection City."

"What was the situation when you left?"

"I managed to put the power plant out of commission at the same time the mutants invaded from the lower city. As soon as the power stopped, all Class Two people fell into a frenzy of head pains and were helpless to defend themselves. I think all died, perhaps within minutes."

"The Class One Rulers—what happened to them?"

"From something a mutant leader said to a group of his people, I believe the mutants invaded the central headquarters. All they found were mutants which they assumed were slaves of the rulers. He said they killed them all because they resisted. It is possible."

"And the invasion, did it succeed?"

"I'm not sure. From what this same leader said, the workers were beginning to fight back, even using weapons they picked off the bodies of the fallen watch guard. My guess is that the mutants, underfed and weak, might find it difficult to overcome the workers if they could develop any organized resistance."

"Then you don't know how it ended?"

"I'm sorry, no."

The man then looked sharply first at me and then at Elissa. "Why did just the two of you, of all the people in Slave City, decide to flee?"

For a moment I thought the question too personal to answer. But what was the harm in giving him a simple explanation?

"I was the only person there who had lived in both the upper and lower cities. I knew the evils of both. I had overheard one of the Class One rulers, a mutant, give orders to have Elissa brought to him for his personal pleasure. At the same time I knew the mutants were planning to invade. I wanted to save her from either fate."

"And what did you expect to find when you crossed the outer wall?"

"Not this," I said as I swept my gaze around the room.

"You mean people living together in the forest?"

"No. I mean normal people and mutants living together in peace and harmony."

XXV

At dinner time that evening, Elissa and I were invited to eat with the family of one of the three men who had found us at the waterfall, a man named Potter. Both the father and mother, and their three beautiful children, two girls and a boy, all seemed to be perfectly normal people. They expressed only warmth and friendliness to us their guests.

The meal was the first that either Elissa or I had where meat was served. She pushed aside the dark brown piece and ate only the vegetables on her plate. I shuddered inwardly for a moment as I put a small portion of the meat in my mouth. The first taste was disgusting. I had the urge to vomit. The mere thought of eating animal flesh was revolting. With effort I chewed and swallowed. In time, perhaps, I could grow to like it. But not now. I finished the other things that were served me.

"Meat is good for you," Potter said.

I politely pushed my plate back. "I'm sorry. I have never eaten meat before."

That evening after dinner while it was still light, Fletcher came to take me on a tour of the settlement. Elissa indicated she would stay at the Potter cabin.

Fletcher and I walked around the perimeter of the village. No walls here I noticed. On two sides, large clearings had been made from the forest and were cultivated into vegetable gardens.

"We are a self-contained community," he explained. "Possibly we are like the early settlers who came into midwest America about 1820 to 1850—well over two centuries ago. We grow what food we need and kill game for meat. The forest has deer and wild pigs and many other animals. We kill only what we need."

"Are there other communities like this in the forest?"

"Yes, there is one about this same size about a day's walk to the northwest and another to the southwest. We visit with each other. There are other groups further away."

"Does the forest cover all the land?"

"Oh, no. This was always forest. All the trees were burned during the war. But they sprang up thicker than ever afterward. No, it is not all forest. I have heard that wherever there were cities, it is just rubble overgrown with weeds and bushes. Slave City is one of the few that had any survivors at all."

I glanced over at him before I asked the question that had been bothering me ever since we arrived. "How are you able to have normal people and mutants live together without hatred and fear of each other?"

Fletcher laughed. "That's something the people in Slave City never found out, isn't it?"

"What's that?"

He laughed again. "After the war of 1999, very few people survived. When those few mated and had children, it was found that some seemed not have been affected at all by the radiation. Others had offspring that had mutated into horribly misshapen creatures. But the thing we discovered after two or three generations was that *all* the survivors had been affected."

"Even those whose children had no physical defects?"

"Yes, even when two completely defect-free people mated, their babies could be malformed. Or two mutants could have apparently perfect young ones. That's why we came to the conclusion that we all carry the taint of that terrible war. And that's why we decided very early to make no distinction."

"I can't believe it," I mused, thinking of Elissa and how she would react to this news.

"Don't take it so hard, Rolf. Here it makes no difference. Those misshapen women at the waterfall must have seemed monstrous to you as a defect-free person. To me they are a welcome part of our community."

"But I am not defect-free," I said. "Elissa is the one without fault."

"And what is yours?"

"Four toes on each foot."

Fletcher laughed. "You are a very handsome young man, Rolf. Here in our community, you would be greatly sought after as a mate. Oh, I admit that those with extreme defects are less admired than those without them. But all are equal here."

He paused and looked questioningly at me. "Would you like to stay with us in our community? We will build a cabin for you and see that it is equipped with the necessary items for living. You and Elissa are welcome to be part of our group."

I shook my head sorrowfully. "I can't speak for Elissa. To persuade her to leave the city, I deceived her. I hadn't meant to but that's how it worked out. I let her think I was her promised mate who was my identical twin brother. She didn't learn of the deception until last evening. She hates me now."

"But you would like to stay?"

"If Elissa will stay, I will stay. I would like it very much."

"Perhaps I could talk to her," Fletcher said. "When she finds out that she too carries the effect of the radiation from her grandparents or great grandparents, she may see how absurd it is to 'hate and fear' mutants as you say the so-called normal people have been doing in Slave City."

"I don't think it will do much good to talk to her. She has received a powerful indoctrination in why she should hate all mutants."

"The only place we have for you two to sleep in is

in the meeting room. Will it help if we put just one sleeping pad there for the two of you?"

"She won't let me touch her. It had better be two separated pads. Or else she'll sleep on the floor as far from me as she can get."

"As you wish. But I believe it would help if you let me talk to her."

"In a few days maybe. But not yet. She is still too stunned by what has happened to her in the last few days."

He led me back to the meeting cabin and I helped him drag two sleeping mats out from a corner closet.

"We use these when we have visitors from the other communities."

He left, saying he would bring Elissa. I sat and waited, my heart beating heavily. How I wanted her in my arms. How I ached to feel her warm, responsive body against mine as I had held her the day before.

She came in with Fletcher. As soon as she saw me she turned to go back out. He stood in her way.

"There is no other place for you," he said gently. He turned and closed the door behind him. A crude candle on the table gave the only illumination.

Without looking at me, Elissa walked to one of the pads. Leaving her tunic on, she slipped down under the single, heavy cover.

I looked at her with longing. Although she made no sounds, I saw she was sobbing. I went over and knelt next to her. I started to put out a comforting hand, then drew it back. Reluctantly I stumbled back to blow out the candle and slip into my own lonely pad.

XXVI

The next morning when I awoke, I found Elissa sitting on a chair next to my pad, looking down at me.

"I have decided," she said.

"What have you decided?"

"I will mate with Fletcher. He is not a mutant. He would make a good mate."

"Does he know this yet?"

"No. I will tell him today. I heard from Potter's woman that Fletcher's mate died last year. I will go to his cabin tonight and sleep with him."

"And I mean nothing to you?"

"Nothing. I loathe you."

"You didn't loathe me two nights ago. You loved me then."

"Not you. I thought you were Ralf. I could never love a mutant. No children of mine will ever bear a mutant strain. I want only defect-free babies. Fletcher is the man I want to be father of my children."

I looked at her, wondering what I should say. Should I tell her what Fletcher had said that *all* the survivors of the war carried, to one degree or another, a radiation taint? That she herself had the potential to bear mutant babies?

Before I could decide what to say, there was a knock on the door. It opened. It was Fletcher carrying two bows and a quiver of arrows.

"I'm going hunting, Rolf. Would you like to come along? I have an extra bow for you."

I glanced back at Elissa. She showed no interest. In fact she had turned her back on us.

"I've never used a bow," I remarked as I held it up to look at it.

"That makes us even," he laughed. "I have never used a laser gun. I brought one of yours with me. You show me how to use it and I'll show you how to use a bow."

I went around and tried to kiss Elissa goodbye. She kept her back turned.

Fletcher spoke to her. "The Potters have kept breakfast ready for you. As for us, Rolf, I have brought a few of your food pellets. I've never eaten one. I'd like to try it."

A few minutes later we were on a path into the woods, a different path than the one we had followed the day before.

How fresh the air smelled. How bright was the sky. How spongy and soft was the turf underfoot. Even after the rebuff by Elissa, I felt that here in nature's land was where I wanted to stay. All my life I had dreamed of her as my mate. Would life suddenly become meaningless without that dream—even here?

When we came to an open glade, Fletcher halted. "This is as good a place as any to test our weapons. First, you with the bow."

He started to string one of the bows and then stopped and put it down. "All right," he said, "something is troubling you. The girl? Didn't she sleep with you last night?"

I smiled wryly. "No. In fact she told me she loathed me. Then, this morning, just before you came, she told me something else . . . something concerning you."

Fletcher's bright eyes lighted up with interest.

"She said that the Potters had told her your mate died last year. She says she is coming to your cabin tonight and plans to sleep with you."

The big man began to laugh and then choked it back.

"If she came to your cabin," I asked, "would you let her in?"

"Of course. I'd be foolish not to. She is a very beautiful girl. Is she really serious about it?"

"I think so, or else she is trying to humiliate me. She said she wouldn't mate with a mutant. She says you are the defect-free kind of man she wants to be father of her children."

"Didn't you tell her that all the descendants of the survivors of the war have some kind of mutation strain? I have myself."

"No, I was about to tell, when you came in. Anyway, coming from me, she wouldn't have believed it. I deceived her once—I thought for her own good—and now she thinks everything I tell her is a lie."

Fletcher looked down at the ground. "What she needs is a good beating. We live a primitive life here. Beating sense into an obstinate woman has always been the right of primitive man."

"Beat her!" I exclaimed. "I couldn't do that."

"The early pioneers all did it. They had to. No woman ever wanted to leave the comforts of the towns back east for the hard struggle for life on the frontier. The men had to beat them to agree to make the trip. It made better mates out of them."

He paused—"Or maybe you ought to beat me."

"What do you mean?"

"Some women became very loving if you beat them when they are stubborn or refuse to let you make love to them. It makes them respect you as a man. Other girls admire the man who defends them against a rival for their attention."

"You can't be serious," I murmured.

"Of course," Fletcher said," you could try both. First, tonight when you go back, order her to sleep with you. When she balks, you will grab her and throw her down on the pad. Rip her clothes off . . . we'll repair them later. Then rape her. I would see to it that no matter how hard she screams, the villagers will not interfere. In fact, when I tell them what was happening, they will probably surround the meeting cabin and fight for a chance to look through the two windows."

"What an animal thing to do," I cried in horror.

"Animal?" Fletcher smiled. "What do you think we all are—gods? We're all animals, Rolf. We were animals to start with. We were animals all through the ages while we clawed our way up from savagery. We were animals when we waged that terrible war in 1999. And we are still animals. You'd be surprised how much good a little slapping around does for a girl."

"No!" I repeated.

"Well then, how about beating me? That's the other course. Let's say she really does come to my cabin to-night. You follow. You plunge through the doorway— I'll leave it unlocked. You are filled with rage. You clench your fists. You yell at me. You rush toward me. I try to defend myself against the rain of blows you will hurl at me. I go down. You kick me. I cry out for mercy. You look down at me and sneer. Don't forget to sneer. Then you take Elissa back to the meeting cabin. Out of respect for your heroics, she will make violent love to you."

"Now I know you are making fun of me," I said.

He shrugged his shoulders. "Well, anyway, those are the two best ideas I have had so far. Maybe I can think of something better later."

"Is it true that your mate died last year?"

His face clouded over. "Yes, and that's one reason why I took you on this hunt today. I want vengeance. So far I've not been able to get it with a bow and arrow. That's the only weapon we have allowed ourselves."

I must have showed my interest because he continued the explanation while he was continuing to string the bow.

"After the great war, the survivors destroyed all weapons. That was seventy years ago. I suppose the people at that time blamed the weapons for all that had happened. All were gathered up wherever found and broken. Now, of course, we realize it was not the weapons but the people themselves—this animal heritage of ours."

"At any rate," he went on, "last year my mate was killed by a wild boar in the field back of the village. It is a dangerous mutation, fully twice as large as the normal wild male pig. Worst of all, it has hide so thick my arrows do not penetrate.

"For a whole year I stalked that beast. Several times I have come close. Twice he nearly got me. I thought before we destroyed the guns you brought with you, we might make one try with your gun."

"So it is true that you have no mate?"

"Oh, three or four of the village girls visit me on occasion. And there's a handsome woman in that community to the northwest who would come and be my mate if I ask her. I have no lack of women."

"Have you no laws against that?"

He looked at me with an amused smile. "There is no law or rule against my hating the boar that killed my mate, why should there be a law against my loving a willing girl? Hate and love are opposites to each other and so the same."

"I don't follow your reasoning."

Fletcher gave me a playful poke. "Perhaps if you don't follow my reasoning, you will follow my plan for killing the boar?"

I nodded.

After handing me the laser gun, he remarked, "I really don't want to learn how to use it. No more, I guess, than you want to learn how to use this bow."

He pointed ahead. "The boar has his den at the edge of a swamp about a half hour's walk from here. He regularly raids our gardens. The villagers are terrified of him and depend on the dogs to warn them when he appears. So far he has killed one other woman and three children. One of my sworn duties, as chief of the community, is to try to kill him. That's why I welcome you and your gun."

"But tell me, Rolf," he continued, "what happens when you use it?"

I held it up for him to see. "On the handle are four small buttons, each a different color. This one at the front, the green one, is for lowest strength, enough to stun a man for about an hour. The second one, the yellow, will stun him for a much longer time and in some cases will result in death. The third button, the blue, will kill anything in its range. The fourth, the red, burns. It cuts through even steel plate. The charge doesn't last too long—only a few seconds—at this top blast."

Fletcher shook his head in wonder. "Just think of the murderous mentality of the men who designed that weapon! Oh, well, let's hope it works against my old enemy, the boar." He paused. "What strength do you plan to use on him?"

"The third. I don't want to start any fires."

For several minutes we moved as silently as we could through the thick forest. Twice I saw graceful deer, although they didn't look quite like those whose pictures I had seen in Milo's books.

"Mutants, too," Fletcher whispered in explanation to my raised eyebrows. "Most of our forest animals are. If we don't get the boar, we'll come back for one of them. The village needs fresh meat." He patted his bow. "But I'll use this on the deer."

At the boar's den, the smell was rank. How much was caused by the animal and how much by the adjoining swamp I could only guess.

"He's out foraging now," Fletcher said. "I think he knows when I come here. Each time he returns from a different direction. I usually get up in that tree over there and wait for him. Shooting the arrows from above, however, is not very effective. His back and sides are like the pieces of metal we often find near the old overgrown highways of the past. I've tried to aim at his eyes or his snout. It has never done any good."

He peered around nervously. "We are very vulnerable here. I'll give you a leg up. Then grab that branch and pull yourself up."

I did as he said. While I was still struggling to reach the safety of the branch, half dangling from it, I heard Fletcher yell.

"Quick!" he shouted.

I turned my head and saw what I realized was the boar plunging toward Fletcher still standing at the base of the tree!

I made an extra heavy effort and pulled myself up. I looked down. Fletcher had dodged behind the tree and thus escaped the first charge of the animal. I leaned over to give him a hand if he could make it up. But the boar had turned with amazing agility and was coming back toward him. He twisted around to the other side of the tree. This time, however, the boar did not charge. Instead it nosed its way toward the helpless victim.

I leaned over still further. I reached into my tunic pocket for the laser gun.

It was gone!

I looked down. There it was on the ground. It must have fallen out while I was climbing.

XXVII

The boar had followed Fletcher around the tree, only an arm's length behind him. In the twisting and turning, the man couldn't even bring up his bow into shooting position.

Suddenly Fletcher darted away from certain death next to the tree to an almost equally certain death in the swamp that lay below us. Or maybe he had seen the gun on the ground and was deliberately diverting the animal away so I could jump down and get it.

I gave one look at the man and beast splashing their way through the shallows. I dropped down.

With the gun in my hand I ran around the tree to the swamp side. Fletcher had turned and was poking weakly with his bow at the head of the boar as it fought its way through the water toward him.

I aimed the gun, pressing the blue button. Perhaps the charge had weakened, or maybe the boar's hide really was as tough as Fletcher had said, but the boar seemed unaffected.

With horrow I watched as man and beast came together. Fletcher seized the animal's huge tusks. The two thrashed around in the water, making so confused a target I dared not fire my gun for fear of hitting the man. Over and over they rolled, the man always desperately holding to the long tusks.

Suddenly the boar gave a convulsive toss of his head and Fletcher went flying into shallower water. This was my chance while the boar was turning to make his final charge. It would have to be the red button, the burn charge.

I aimed and fired.

There was an explosion of flames and smoke where the boar had been. Pushing the gun back into my pocket, I plunged into the swamp. Fletcher was already sinking below the surface. Putting my hands under his armpits, I dragged him to the more solid ground. He was unconscious. I glanced around. A few weeds and bushes nearby were burning, but the fires soon flickered out. There was no sign or the boar.

Fletcher was still breathing and his heart was beating as I examined his wounds. I tore strips of cloth from his already badly torn tunic and bandaged the worst of the gashes in his body.

I debated in my mind whether or not to run to the village for help. But I did not like the idea of leaving him alone. There might be other wild beasts.

For several hours I watched over him, looking for any sign of his return to consciousness. Finally he roused up on one elbow and looked up at me. "The boar is dead?"

I nodded. He sighed and slipped off again into sleep.

It was late afternoon when he stirred and tried to stand up. At first he could hardly stay erect. Then he announced in a shaky voice that he was ready to start back.

Every step was one of torture for him. I did the best I could to support his big body. I was amazed at his endurance. In fact it seemed that he was stronger at the end than when we started.

Night was just beginning to descend when we entered the village. Several of the men helped me get Fletcher into his cabin. He seemed glad enough to slip into his sleeping pad and let us cover him.

"The boar is dead," I told the men who had helped. "It nearly got him. Is there anyone who could wash off his wounds and put clean bandages on him?"

One of the men spoke up. "I'll send my daughter

over to tend him." He shook his head wonderingly. "So Fletcher finally got the boar!"

I waited in the cabin until a young woman came. She was a healthy-looking comely girl of about my own age. I could see no mutant defects on her.

"I'll stay here and take care of him tonight," she said. "They tell me he killed the boar."

I realized then the importance to Fletcher to be thought by the villagers as the slayer of the boar. I remembered what he had said about it being one of his main duties as community chief.

"Yes," I said. "He led it into the waters of the swamp and drowned it."

The girl's eyes turned to the sleeping man on his mat. "He fought it with his bare hands in the water?"

I knew the girl would spread the story the next day, so I added a few embellishments to my report, skirting the truth only slightly. "I was in a tree. My gun had fallen out of my pocket and was on the ground. The only way I could get it was for Fletcher to draw the boar off into the water. It was impossible for him to use his bow. When the boar plunged in after him, he seized its tusks and tried to push its head under the water. They thrashed about so violently I didn't dare fire my gun while they were so close together."

The girl's eyes were wide with excitement. "And then what?"

"The next thing I knew the boar was stopping its attack. Fletched had drowned it. Then he pushed the dead animal off into deep water. He was so bruised and exhausted he collapsed. He is a great man."

"Yes, I know," the girl said.

"One thing you must know," I added. "He had a terrible struggle. He may not remember exactly what happened. He may even think I helped kill the boar. If he says that, tell him I swear he drowned it with his own hands. I fired my gun once but the beam went wide."

The girl went over and lifted the cover from Fletcher's bruised body. A moment later she was bringing water to cleanse his cuts.

I turned and left the cabin.

Now—Elissa!

I had had one fight today. I did not want another. At least she had not gone to Fletcher's cabin as she had threatened to do.

How would she receive me? I smiled as I thought of Fletcher's suggestion that I treat her like any pioneer woman. I suspect that he was more than half serious about it.

I wondered how loving she would become if I really did beat her? It might work. Or it could drive her away from me forever. What I was counting on were the many sound arguments for her to realize that her place really was with me. I loved her. Our bodies had found pleasure in each other. We were strangers together among these forest dwellers. Most of all, I was beginning to see the truth of Fletcher's statement that all descendants of the war's survivors shared, to some degree or other, the mutant taint. Even Elissa herself.

No, I would not nor could not beat her to make her come into my arms. Rape was unthinkable. I wanted only an eager and willing girl, as she had been two nights before at the base of the wall.

A warmth and a glow filled me as I reached out to open the door to the meeting cabin. If only, during the day, she had fought her own personal battle, and had decided that what she had left behind was truly Slave City . . . that what life beyond the walls offered was freedom from the hatreds and fears of that dread place . . . and most of all that I offered her love.

If only. . . .

180

I pushed open the door. The candle on the table was not burning. "Elissa, are you there?" I called.

When there was no answer, I felt in the corner where they had put my bag of supplies. The bag was gone.

"Elissa," I cried out, "where are you?"

Frantically I felt all around the room. Elissa was gone!

XXVIII

When I was finally convinced that Elissa had fled, taking the bag of supplies with her, I hurried over to the Potter cabin.

"Do you know where Elissa is?" I asked Potter when he came at my hard knocking.

One of his little daughters spoke up from behind him. "I saw her go down toward the waterfall just after lunch. She said she was going to take a bath in the pool."

"Was she carrying a bag?"

"Yes, she said she wanted to wash out some clothes."

I groaned.

"What's the matter?" Poter asked.

"I'm afraid that Elissa is trying to go back to the city."

"Go back to Slave City! That would be madness."

I held out my hands in a gesture of despair. "Could you, or is there anybody in the village to lead me back to the wall?"

"At night! And anyway, if she left this noon, she has a seven or eight hour start. You'll never be able to catch up to her."

"I could try. I must try. Will you help?"

He looked out at the moonless night sky. "It's very dark in the forest. Everything looks different. You don't know what you ask."

"I'll go alone," I said as I turned away. I had gone only a few steps when he called to me. "Wait. I'll get my neighbor, Miller. We'll guide you."

I waited until he returned with the man he called Miller. He and Potter were the other two men who had been with Fletcher when they had surprised me at the waterfall.

I told them of my fears that Elissa had fled back to the city. Miller, too, said he thought we were too late. If she had left the village at noon, she would have reached the wall many hours ago. She might even be at the inner wall by now.

I groaned at the thought of her reaching the inner wall before I could stop her. What kind of horrors awaited her in the city? If the mutants had won out, she would be fortunate to be killed rather than be taken as a female slave to serve one of the creatures. If the Class Three workers had won, what kind of life would she have among them? I knew she hadn't believed me when I said Ralf was dead. How crushed she would be when she learned the truth.

In the dark, Potter spoke to his neighbor. "There's no use trying to go through the forest at night. Let's take the old auto highway. It's further, but we can go faster."

"The auto highway?" I asked, wondering what he meant.

"Yes, in the old days before the war, an auto expressway ran through these woods toward the city. In seventy years, it's completely broken up and useless for travel. Weeds and grass and even small trees have sprung up along its length. But it's more open than the forest paths."

About ten minutes later the two men led me out to what I would have assumed was merely a slash through the trees. It was too dark to see anything more than that it was more open than being in the woods. Immediately we set off at a steady jog. Occasionally we stumbled over broken places in the roadway, or even tangles of vines or roots. But we made good time, nevertheless. At length we stopped.

"The old highway ends here," Potter said. "When the

wall was built, all sections beyond here were removed. The wall is only a few minutes ahead."

"How far is it to the ladder I used the other day?"

"It's about a quarter hour to the right. We'll go that far with you. We won't go over the wall. Nothing could make us go over to the other side."

I smiled to myself. To think I had supposed the forest dwellers had used the ladder to go over and steal food! There were so many things I had been wrong about.

We made our way along the base of the wall to where the ladder still leaned against it. Had Elissa found the way? Had she been able to climb up and use the tree to get down on the other side?

I thanked the two men and said I had no choice but to go after the girl. I told them I hoped I could bring her back with me.

I crawled up the ladder. A few minutes later I had managed to get over to the tree and slide down. I searched the sheltered spot where we had spent the night. There was no sign of her. What if she had not been able to find her way through the woods? No, I had to assume that she had reached this point and gone on.

I tried to look out across the fields. I could see nothing. She probably had arrived here some time before dark. Perhaps she had chosen to go on toward the city in the approaching darkness rather than wait for daylight and my possibly finding her.

I waded across the irrigation ditch. Fixing my direction by the stars, I headed for the city. In the darkness, I estimated it might take two or three hours to cross the fields.

Tired as I was, I stumbled on through fields of grain, rows of tall corn stalks, cabbage patches, and even across empty stretches only recently plowed. Sometimes

184

the growing things were over my head and I had trouble pushing through. Always, I kept my directions.

Almost without warning, I came to the tall inner wall. Which way to go? For an hour I felt my way along the base of the wall. I passed three control stations but they were not the one I had entered by. At all of them the doors were closed and locked.

In despair I turned around and wearily retraced my steps. For another two hours I moved in that direction. By now a dimness was showing on the eastern horizon. In the faint light I saw another station ahead. It had to be the right one. Soon full daylight would be here.

A short distance from the wall was a field of corn. I scurried into it, and under its protection, ran parallel to the wall. Just as I reached opposite the control station, I could see that the door was swinging open as I had left it.

At that same instant I saw Elissa!

She, too, apparently had been waiting for enough light to see her way into the station. Even as I shoved the stubble away from me so that I could call out to her, she stumbled forward toward the open door.

Just as she reached it, she stopped, screamed and staggered back. Standing in the doorway, not an arm's length from her, was a hideous monstrosity of a mutant. He was grinning as he reached out for the screaming, cowering girl.

He never saw me as I ran up. Pushing Elissa aside, I shoved the laser gun up against the mutant's chest. I pressed the red button. Nothing happened. In despair I pressed the blue, then the yellow, then the green. In killing the boar I had used up the charge?

By this time the mutant had realized he had an enemy in front of him. Fortunately he was slow-witted and awkward. His arms flailed at me. I ducked and came up into his midsection with the top of my head. He went backward struggling to keep his balance. Again

I hit him as hard as I could across the throat. It was a blow Milo had taught me. He grunted in pain and turned to try to escape my wild attack. He ran back into the station and out through the passageway in the inner wall.

I made a quick glance around. The three guards were still where they had fallen when the power was shut off. They had not been touched. I went back to the door that led to the fields. Elissa was nowhere in sight. I called out.

A moment later she made her way slowly out of the shelter of the tall corn stalks. She seemed in a daze. I walked up to her and took her arm.

"Elissa, we're going home now."

She shook her head.

Seizing her hand, I pulled her behind me. It was hard going. And minute by minute, I was getting more and more angry.

Letting her rest only when I could see she couldn't take another step, it was mid-morning when we reached the outer wall. We stopped there to rest again.

"Elissa," I said, "after we have rested, we are going over the wall. I'm too tired to carry you. You will have to help yourself."

Again she shook her head.

For an hour we sat there in silence. When I finally spoke, it was in a low, gentle voice—

"I know how you feel, Elissa. Both our lives have changed. You must accept the change."

She kept her eyes downcast as I went on—

"You must realize that Ralf is dead. I saw him dying. All Class Two people died when the power was shut off. He was my twin brother. I loved him. I tried to warn him about the invasion. His last motion, as he was dying, was to urge me to save you."

I paused, wondering what more I could say to convince her of Ralf's death.

186

"Going back to Resurrection City was wrong, Elissa. You saw that mutant. That probably means that the mutants won the battle. I hate to think what they are doing to the women they find. I hate to think what would have happened to you if you had gone into that control station a moment earlier.

"There is nothing in Ressurection City for us, Elissa. It's a lost city. Out here, where the forest dwellers live, is the only place where we can find hapiness. Here is where all people live together without fear and without hatred.

"The human race has always had mutants. It is part of our evolution, like taking one step backward for every two steps forward. A mutant is often a breakthrough to something better. In the days before the war, animal breeders used it to get superior horses, cattle and dogs.

"Fletcher told me something I think you should know, my darling. He said that after three full generations since the war, they have found that all descendants of those who survived the war carry the taint of mutancy. That is why they can live together in peace. No one is better than any other."

I stood up and faced the girl as she sat, her legs doubled up under her.

"According to what he said, even you, Elissa, carry the possibility of bearing mutant children."

For a moment she just sat there. Then suddenly she jumped to her feet and ran toward the irrigation ditch. When I seized her, she hit at me with her clenched fists, screaming, "I'm not a mutant! You lie to me! You've always lied to me!"

I started to shake her. I realized that was doing no good. She was kicking and hitting at me with a wild crazy kind of fury.

What had Fletcher advised? Beat her? Well, I had tried everything else.

187

"I hate you! I hate you!" she was screaming at me, tears streaming down her face.

"Well, I don't hate you," I shouted back at her as a blinding rage seized me. All the frustrations and fears and terrors of the past few days welled up in me. I wanted to hurt her, to break her obstinate, stubborn willfulness.

I reached for her. She struggled against me as I pulled her to the ground and straddled her twisting body.

"You're going to listen to me, Elissa. Fletcher told me I should beat you. He said we are all pioneers out here and that is the only way pioneer women were made to be obedient and loving to their mates. He said I should beat you and then rape you."

I looked down at her flushed face, her eyes twin fires of anger, her lips tightly compressed.

"But I won't do that to you, Elissa. I want you as you were that night before we entered the forest."

My anger ebbed as I looked at her lying helplessly below me. Slowly I got up. I moved away from her.

"And so, my darling, you have your choice. You can go back to Resurrection City and almost certain death. Or you can go with me across the wall and be my loving mate."

She simply stared back at me.

I turned and headed for the tree we had used before for reaching the top of the wall. I moved carefully along the tree limb and leaped to the wall top. Still without looking back, I strode along to where the ladder stood. Slowly, my spirits low, I climbed down and headed for the forest. Only when I reached it did I look back. There was no sign of Elissa.

Perhaps I was expecting too much. After all, her whole life had been in a training school dedicated to making her hate and fear mutants. In her eyes I was a mutant and she was not.

For two hours I sat waiting, hoping against hope to see her come along the wall top. Just when I was debating in my mind whether to go back to look for her or go on to the village, Fletcher suddenly appeared.

"You should be in bed," I exclaimed in surprise.

"It takes more than a few cuts and bruises to keep me down. When Potter told me about your following Elissa, I thought I'd better see if I could give you any help."

He looked at me pensively. "I gather you didn't find her."

"I found her. She is on the other side of the wall— either sitting there or on her way back to her death in Resurrection City."

"Didn't you beat her as I suggested?"

"No, I couldn't."

"Rolf, you're a fool. If you won't go after her, I will. And if I do, she'll be mine."

I jumped to my feet. "You're still weak from the boar fight, Fletcher, and I won't fight you. But if anyone gets her, it will be me."

"Hurt or not, I'll fight you for her, Rolf!"

He swung at me wildly. I stepped back. Again he came at me. Again I dodged, but a bit too late. His fist hit me a glancing blow at the side of the head that sent me reeling.

For the second time that day a rage sprang up in me. As before when I had thrown Elissa violently to the ground, this time I plunged toward Fletcher with all my pent-up anger suddenly released. I hit at him with my doubled-up fists. I felt his blows on me. I even felt an animalistic joy as I saw him stagger back under my attack. I was driving him back. I was beating him down. It was good to be winning. Winning! Winning!

"No more," he cried out as I stood over him.

I saw his eyes turn and look back toward the wall. Elissa had descended the ladder and was standing at the base of the wall staring at us. She took a step toward us. Then she ran up and stood next to me.

Fletcher looked up at her and groaned, a somewhat forced groan of despair.

As I put my arm around her shoulders, I glanced down at Fletcher. Behind her back he was smiling broadly at me. And I knew exactly why he was smiling. . . .

Important Questionnaire

We value your opinion. Please give us your reactions to **Walls Within Walls** in order to help us make this new series of LASER Books the very best in exciting reading entertainment. Your FREE BOOK, **Seeds of Change**, will be sent to you immediately upon receipt of this completed questionnaire. (Please check (✓) the appropriate boxes.)

1. What prompted you to buy **Walls Within Walls**?
   ☐ Cover Design ☐ Story Outline ☐ Price

2. Did you enjoy this LASER Book?
   ☐ Yes   ☐ No

3. Were you sufficiently pleased to purchase other LASER Books?
   ☐ Yes   ☐ No

4. What type of stories do you generally read?
   ☐ Sci. Fiction   ☐ Mystery & Suspense
   ☐ Westerns   ☐ Adventure
   ☐ Other (please specify)

5. At what store did you purchase this novel?
   ☐ Book   ☐ Cigar   ☐ Supermkt.
   ☐ Drug   ☐ Department   ☐ Chain

6. Please indicate your general age group.
   ☐ Under 20 yrs. ☐ 30 - 50 yrs.
   ☐ 20 - 30 yrs.   ☐ Over 50 yrs.

For your **FREE LASER BOOK**, MAIL YOUR COMPLETED QUESTIONNAIRE TO:

Seeds of Change
LASER READER SERVICE
M.P.O. Box 788, Niagara Falls, N.Y. 14302

*Cdn. Residents: Send to Stratford, Ont., Canada

Name...
Address......................................
City/Town....................................
State/Prov...........Zip/Postal Code.......